"If you don't stir that," Roanna admonished me, indicating the pan on the stove, "we're going to have a fat, shapeless omelet instead of scrambled eggs."

"Sorry."

I didn't hear the door open, just felt the wet blast of air. I turned around, pan in one hand, wooden spoon in the other. My heart jumped sharply.

"Hello girls," he said. The gun he held was very familiar to me. A snub-nosed, double-action Smith & Wesson .38 automatic. Practical, deadly, and efficient.

LOOKING FOR NAIAD?

Buy our books at
www.naiadpress.com

or call our toll-free number
1-800-533-1973

or by fax (24 hours a day)
1-850-539-9731

Murder Undercover

A Denise Cleever
THRILLER

Claire McNab

THE NAIAD PRESS, INC.
1999

Printed in the United States of America on acid-free paper
First Edition

Editor: Lila Empson
Cover designer: Bonnie Liss (Phoenix Graphics)
Typesetter: Sandi Stancil

Library of Congress Cataloging-in-Publication Data

McNab, Claire.
    Murder undercover: A Denise Cleever thriller / by Claire McNab.
        p.   cm.
    ISBN 1-56280-259-3   (alk. paper)
    I. Title.
    PS3563.C3877M87   1999
    813'.54—dc21   99-18394
                                                                              CIP

FICTION

12/99

For darling Sheila

and for our Soph

Acknowledgments

My thanks to the exceptional Sandi Stancil and the wonderful Lila Empson.

ABOUT THE AUTHOR

CLAIRE McNAB is the author of eleven Detective
Inspector Carol Ashton mysteries: *Lessons in Murder,*
Fatal Reunion, Death Down Under, Cop Out, Dead
Certain, Body Guard, Double Bluff, Inner Circle, Chain
Letter, Past Due and *Set Up*. She has written two
romances, *Under the Southern Cross* and *Silent Heart,*
and has co-authored a self-help book, *The Loving*
Lesbian, with Sharon Gedan. *Murder Undercover,* is
the first Denise Cleever thriller.

In her native Australia she is known for her crime
fiction, plays, children's novels and self-help books.

Now permanently resident in Los Angeles, Claire
teaches fiction writing in the UCLA Extension Writers'
Program. She makes it a point to return to Australia
once a year to refresh her Aussie accent.

Prologue

The clay pigeon arched over the turquoise sea. The stocky tourist, his sweat-stained orange T-shirt sticking to his thick chest, blazed away with both barrels of the shotgun. Untouched, the clay plate splashed into the water.

"Aw, jeez!" He ripped off his ear protection and wiped a beefy forearm across his forehead. "There's something wrong with the sights on this gun."

Under the meager shade thrown by a stand of coconut palms, several of the group waiting to shoot chuckled at his statement. "Yeah, sure, Morrie," said a whippet-thin man also wearing an orange T-shirt. Across his narrow chest, glaring purple letters declared ABSCOUND INDUSTRIES.

"My turn," said an angular woman with a mean mouth. "Move it, willya?" As Morrie hesitated, reluctant to leave the shooting platform, she broke open the shotgun she held and inserted two heavy red cartridges. Snapping it shut, she began to mount the two wooden steps to the platform.

Afterward, witnesses gave conflicting details, but all agreed that she had stumbled, her shotgun had discharged, and the side of Morrie's head had vanished in a spray of blood, bone and brain tissue.

The wooden platform shook as the body collapsed. "Oh, my God," someone said.

Afterward, no one thought to mention to the authorities the jarring way the woman had turned to the appalled audience and snapped with peevish anger, "It was an accident. You all saw. You'll say it was an accident."

As if there had been any doubt.

CHAPTER ONE

"Got a challenge for you, Den." Eddie Trebonus planted his elbows on the cane-and-Formica bar counter and smirked at me. "You know how to make a Baltimore bracer?"

I gave him my best bright smile. "Coming right up." Up to this point in time, I'd quite liked Americans, but Eddie was a poor advertisement for his nation. Not only did he have the worst taste in clothes — today he was wearing a brown-and-yellow striped top, bilious green Bermuda shorts, and white socks

3

with his sandals — but he also had a flabby body and thick, blotchy skin that was peeling from too much tropical sun.

I've always found American accents pleasant, but Eddie had a kind of metallic twang that put my teeth on edge. "You sure you know how to make a Baltimore bracer, Den?"

I bit back a retort. If there's one thing I can't stand, it's having my name shortened. Along with my uniform of white shorts and a hibiscus-flower shirt — the choice of pink, yellow, orange, red or a particularly hectic purple — all staff had to wear an identifying tag. I tapped the bright pink hibiscus-shaped badge on my right breast. "The name's Denise."

"Denise, eh?" He said loudly, apparently playing to a nonexistent crowd. "And what's the left one called?" He chortled at his own joke, looking around to see if anyone else appreciated his humor. As it was ten on Friday morning, the Tropical Heat Cocktail Lounge only had a few people scattered around its glass-and-cane tables. Not one of them showed any interest in Eddie's idea of humor, although Biddy Gallagher, a sinewy, tanned woman who'd won my admiration with her astonishing ability to consume hard liquor, did snap the paper she was reading with obvious irritation.

This guy was getting to be more than tiresome. I'd been behind the bar for a week, and Eddie had been one of my first customers. Since then he'd turned up regularly to request a host of obscure cocktails. Well, they were obscure to me, but then, I'd only been a bartender for a short time, no matter what my résumé said, and the crash course I'd done in drink recipes

4

wasn't much help when someone like Eddie Trebonus was doing his best to catch me out.

The other employee with me, Pete, was a fair dinkum bartender, so I'd tried to steer the Yank in his direction, but blasted Eddie, his rubbery lips stretched in a suggestive smile, always insisted on giving his drink orders to me.

Pete looked like what he was — a genuinely nice guy. He had a pleasant, nondescript face, usually warmed by a cheeky smile, and a neat, compact body. I hadn't been able to hide from Pete that I wasn't half as experienced as I'd claimed to be, but he'd been a good sport and had only grinned when he caught me in the back quickly flicking through a paperback titled *The Home Bartender's Guide to Every Drink* after my first encounter with Eddie. That time Eddie had requested, leering appropriately, a temptation cocktail. I'd tried to steer him onto the Aylmer Resort's own drink, the tropical whacker, as I'd been comprehensively instructed on how to make this lethal combination of fruit juices, rum, brandy and gin. No such luck. Eddie had been determined to embarrass me, an ambition he was still pursuing.

"Baltimore bracer," Eddie repeated, seating himself on one of the cane bar stools. "Don't you hurry, now, Den. Wouldn't want you to make a mistake."

I contemplated hitting him, hard. That would wipe the stupid grin off his face. Of course, it would also blow my chances of continuing undercover, so I said, "You're a challenge!" with just the right tone of playful respect.

Eddie snickered. "Yeah," he said. "A lot more than you know."

Convinced that he was about to add that he could show me a good time, baby, I hastened around the back of the bar to consult my cocktail guide. Pete, who was getting a replacement bottle of Baileys Irish Cream, said, "Let me save you the trouble, love. It's a measure of brandy, measure of anisette, throw in an egg white, shake it up with ice and whack it in a stemmed glass."

It sounded revolting to me, but then, I only drink beer, and that not very often.

Eddie was waiting like a fat, sunburnt toad, chewing peanuts with his mouth open. I put the Baltimore bracer ingredients in a shaker, added ice, and did a good imitation of a demented maraca player. Straining the results into a glass, I placed it in front of Eddie with a flourish. "Your cocktail."

Then, sighing to myself, I got down to business. "You're not here for the convention, then?" I said, knowing there was always some convention underway at Aylmer Resort, usually drawing overseas guests. That was part of the reason I was there.

"Nah. Strictly a vacation." He leaned closer. "Looking for a little action."

It wasn't clear to me if this was a question or a statement. Either way I was repelled. I soothed myself by nonchalantly wiping the bar, a skill I'd learned from watching countless bartenders in countless movies. Lifting the carved wooden peanut bowl, the contents severely depleted by Eddie's depredations, I swept my damp cloth over the spot. "Action?" I said vaguely. "You'd mean windsurfing, snorkeling, skeet shooting, that sort of thing."

"Skeet shooting? You talking about clay pigeons? No way are you going to get me doing *that*. Didn't you hear what happened to that guy? Someone blew his head off!"

"Did you know him?" I asked casually.

"Who? The guy?" Eddie shook his head. "Nah, he was here with a convention group. Electronics, or something." He took a gulp of his Baltimore bracer and swished it around his mouth before swallowing it.

For a moment I'd been afraid he was going to spit it out like mouthwash. Hiding my distaste for everything that Eddie said or did, I said, "I've seen you with the Aylmers, and I thought you must be a friend of the family."

Eddie was pleased with my observation. "Yeah," he said, "they don't socialize with just anybody."

That was true. The Aylmer dynasty has been a force in Australian politics and business for well over a century, and counted the other rich and famous as their friends and relatives. Aylmer Island, inside the Great Barrier Reef, and only a short flight or boat ride from the mainland, had been deeded to the first robber baron Aylmer in the late nineteenth century and, apart from a small holiday shacks, had been left in its natural state until fifteen years ago, when one branch of the family had developed it as a luxury resort.

"Don't suppose you've noticed," said Eddie, smacking his lips, "but the daughter, Roanna Aylmer, is a real looker."

Of course I'd noticed. And he was selling Roanna short. She was sensational. Slim, tall, dark-haired and with a rebellious get-out-of-my-way look I found instantly attractive.

"I hadn't noticed," I said.

Over Eddie's shoulder I saw with surprise that the

subject of Eddie's leering comment had just strolled into the cocktail lounge and was heading our way.

Eddie, oblivious to this, nodded wisely at me. "And Roanna's hot for it. Trust me, I know."

"Who's hot, Eddie?" said Roanna behind him.

The whole cocktail thing instantly became worth it, just to see Eddie's face flush an unbecoming scarlet.

"Hello," he croaked, twisting around to look at her. "I didn't see you come in."

"Obviously."

There was a long silence, one that I enjoyed and Eddie clearly didn't.

"I'd better be going," he said at last. He tossed back the last of his drink. Nodded to Roanna, and slid off his chair. "Be seeing you."

She watched him go, then turned back to me. "What do you think of Eddie?"

Difficult. Eddie was a guest of the Aylmer family, and I was just an employee, and a new one at that. I tried a blank expression and a minimal shrug as a response.

"I asked you a question," Roanna said.

"A trick one."

She raised one eyebrow, a capability I'd never been able to master. It was clear she was going to wait until she got an answer, so I said, "I reckon if I say what I really think, I'll get fired. And if I lie . . ." I grinned at her. "Why, I wouldn't be true to myself."

There was a snort of laughter behind me. "We couldn't have that, could we?" said Pete.

Roanna was smiling too. She was also looking at me with a speculative expression. I'd surprised her, and that was good. My instructions were to infiltrate the Aylmer family if I could, and I had been shuddering at the thought that Eddie Trebonus might be my only way in. Roanna was more than preferable.

I said, "Can I get you something to drink?"

She hesitated, then gave a quick nod, to herself more than to me. "Lemon squash," she said, then added, "Please."

While I was filling a glass with crushed ice, Pete, who was cutting lime wedges, said softly out of the corner of his mouth, "Nice going, Denise, but watch out. She can be trouble."

He already knew that I preferred women to men. Hell, I didn't just prefer them, men had been totally excluded from my romantic fantasies since my late teens. Pete had cheerfully put the hard word on me during our first shift together, but had been quite unfazed when I'd set him straight. "Too bad," he'd said, grinning. "I've always had a weakness for blond, athletic women."

In truth, I was really a sort of dark honey blond, but I'd lightened my hair for this undercover job, and gone back to wearing my contact lenses full time. As for his reference to the athletic, too much desk work had softened me up, and I'd had to spend hours in the gym getting fully fit and bringing my self-defense skills up to a reasonable standard.

"How is she trouble?" I whispered back.

He grinned at me. "Goes through hearts like a hot knife through butter."

I plunked down a hibiscus coaster in front of Roanna Aylmer and set the lemon squash on it. She was watching me with a disconcerting dark stare, which I ignored. "Peanuts?" I said.

She peered at the bowl that Eddie had depleted. Wrinkling her nose, she said, "Have you got something better?"

"I'll have a look."

I disappeared to my refuge behind the shelves of brightly labeled bottles. Bar staff were told to provide upmarket nuts for obviously upmarket customers, and I guessed Roanna fitted the bill. I dug out a large container that declared itself MIXED SUPERIOR NUTS and put a generous scoop into a wooden bowl painted with tropical birds of garish plumage.

Pete put his head around the edge of the shelves. "Can you hold the fort for a mo? I've got to get some stuff out of the storage shed." I nodded, and he disappeared out the back door.

My ASIO briefings hadn't given me much information on Roanna, other than that she had a degree in computing but she'd never used it. She was the youngest daughter of Moreen and George Aylmer and was said to be wild, though no details were given. There was another daughter, Greta, who was considerably older and who had married and was living in Broome, Western Australia. The male side of the family was reinforced with two sons, Harry and Quint, who helped run the resort. I hadn't spoken to either, although both were quite presentable, if you liked the sulky, arrogant look. I hadn't up till now, but their sister had it down pat, and on her it seemed quite engaging.

I slid the nuts next to her untouched lemon squash. "Anything else?"

"Why are you working here?" Roanna said. No beating around the bush for her.

"I love the tropics."

10

She gave me an unbelieving smile. "Oh yeah?"

At a table behind her, Biddy Gallagher folded her paper and slapped it down. "Jeez!" Biddy said, glaring in my direction. "What's a woman got to do to get a drink around here?"

"Coming."

"Let Pete do it," said Roanna.

I made a mental note that she knew Pete's name. Perhaps his remark that Roanna was trouble came from personal experience. "Pete isn't here," I said, lifting the leaf in the bar. "He's gone to get supplies."

I went over to Biddy, who was tapping impatiently with bright scarlet nails. "Took your time," she said severely. "Double Scotch on the rocks." She grinned. "I suggest you go light on the rocks and heavy on the Haig."

When I turned back to the bar, the bowl of superior nuts and the lemon squash sat all alone. Roanna had gone.

CHAPTER TWO

My first shift of the day ended. I was expected back for the boisterous evening period, where every night was party night, but in the meantime I had the afternoon to myself. I set off for the staff quarters, strolling through the lush beauty of the tropical gardens. A small army of gardeners rushed out at dawn to keep the burgeoning vegetation in check, then disappeared before guests could see them tampering with perfection. I stopped at my favorite spot, a little clearing hidden from the path. There was a dark green wooden bench situated to give a view of the water, but I'd never seen anyone else sitting on it. I sat down to enjoy the moment of tranquillity before I faced the exuberance of the staff quarters.

This was the first time I'd seen Roanna Aylmer in the flesh, although, like all new staff, I'd had to sit through an orientation video, which introduced each member of the Aylmer family. The rest of the family had made an effort to smile at the camera, but Roanna had gazed coolly out of the screen, as though nothing to do with the resort related to her. The video featured patriarch George Aylmer's voice extolling the wonderful qualities of Aylmer Resort Island, followed by an outline of staff duties — various individuals were shown being helpful, smiling, and otherwise appearing as perfect employees — and finally a list of things staff did not do. These forbidden items included having any close personal relationship with a guest, failing to wear a name tag, and neglecting to present a smiling face and a helpful manner at all times.

I shrugged off any thoughts of my duties, and enjoyed the moment. It was close to heaven in this little hidden nook. A brilliant blue butterfly flapped nonchalantly by, and the wind rustled the leaves of blossom-laden shrubs, through whose branches I could catch glimpses of the pastel water and a crescent of pale beach. Aylmer Resort was situated on the quintessential tropical island. Palm trees swayed in the cooling breeze that blew off the surface of the blue-green water lapping dazzlingly white coral sand. There were no dramatic crashing waves, as the Pacific Ocean spent its force on the Great Barrier Reef, which ran as a protective barricade down much of the coast of Queensland.

Half the island was rain forest, stocked like some

vast film set with brilliantly colored tropical birds, cycads and ferns of every type, which grew like giant weeds in the gloom under the thick green canopy formed by trees stretching ever upward toward the light. I'd been delighted to find vines draped picturesquely from branch to branch. Less invitingly, an extraordinary range of insects of daunting size shared the island with us, and I'd been told there were leeches in some damp areas. The thought of leeches made me shudder.

The resort's guest accommodation was based on one word: *luxury*. The choice was between an individual cabana nestled in the greenery near the water or a suite in the five-star hotel set into the side of a gentle hill. Only two stories high, the hotel was artfully hidden by skillful landscaping, so that from the sea it was almost invisible. The gardens were extensive, and there was even a maze, small but puzzling, that had emergency telephones at intervals in case some hapless visitor failed to find his or her way out.

My stomach growled, so I gave a last glance to a jewellike hummingbird suckling at a huge yellow blossom and reluctantly resumed my walk. In case anyone should think to wander in the direction of the staff housing, stern notices announced STAFF ONLY PAST THIS POINT at the entrance to the driveway that curved away so that even the most determined guest would be unable to view the buildings, which was a good thing, since they would have been an unwelcome shock. In stark contrast to the comfortable affluence of the rest of the resort, the staff quarters were strictly utilitarian.

Not for us the sumptuous interiors, the king-size

beds, the private verandas and balconies. In fact, I wouldn't have been surprised if the initial plans for staff housing had called for something like military barracks. Fortunately someone had decided that a happy staff needed individual rooms. Mine was, as far as I could see, identical to everyone else's. The walls were beige, the ceiling off-white, with a ceiling fan positioned in the center. A generic air-conditioner blocked the bottom of the narrow window, the top half being covered with a flimsy accordion blind, again in the ubiquitous beige. Cheap and functional furniture had been selected: a metal-frame single bed, a simple dresser with three drawers that doubled as a bedside table, a gooseneck lamp, a desk with a couple of shelves set above it, one beige plastic chair, a curtained hanging space for clothes. A beige-and-brown circular mat covered the floor near the desk, its bland coloring picked up by the cotton bedspread. After only a few days there, I'd become obsessively anti-beige, in fact, I'd vowed to myself that any future home of mine would be totally beige-free.

I vaguely remembered that some famous architect had said that every fully functional building had its own beauty. That architect would have been captivated by our ablutions block. The showers and toilets — one side male, the other female — and the laundry room with a row of washers and dryers, were located in a gray concrete structure with a flat roof. The building was constructed so that every area could be hosed out with a high-powered jet of water. This cleansing happened at five o'clock every morning.

The ablutions block brought back memories of roughing it on camping excursions when I was young, and I recalled my mother's dire warnings about how every shower stall was guaranteed to harbor the fungus causing athlete's foot. At that time I'd always obediently worn my rubber flip-flops to shower, and I rather regretted that I didn't have them with me now.

The most popular areas in the staff buildings were the communal kitchen and the adjacent recreation room. Both rooms, predictably, were painted beige. The kitchen had the usual standard equipment of electric stoves, microwaves, sinks and benches, plus several industrial-size refrigerators. These were always bursting with food and drink. Everyone labeled their possessions, but there were constant arguments about what bottle belonged to whom, and accusations about stolen milk and pilfered food.

Half the recreation room was set up with tables for dining. The other half had a television set that was always turned on, ancient table-tennis equipment, and an assortment of chairs that seemed to have been collected at a variety of jumble sales.

We weren't supposed to eat in our rooms, but of course everyone did, and I had arrived with a stock of exotic goodies that could be used to lure people into conversations, working on the principle that it would be difficult to clam up on someone who was being bountiful. It was tiring, but I had already established myself as the most pleasant, cheerful, gregarious person possible, knowing that staff members would gossip if encouraged, and that they could be a valuable source of information about the Aylmers and their activities.

Of course there was one problem with being so outgoing, and that was the expectation that I might be interested in the bed-hopping that seemed to be a major form of recreation. No one seemed alarmed about my sexual orientation, information that Pete obviously had let slip at the earliest opportunity. Almost everyone seemed good-natured, younger than me, and relentlessly energetic. I was rather flattered to receive veiled propositions from several coworkers, both male and female, but I let it be known that underneath my smiling exterior I was nursing a seriously dented heart, so I was not ready for any relationship, however fleeting.

I was peering into a refrigerator and debating if it would be more profitable to walk all the way back to the main restaurant in the resort, where there was a small staff dining room at the back near the kitchen, when Seb slapped me on the shoulder. "Den!" he said. "Whatcha up to?"

"It's Denise," I corrected him, with little hope that he'd pay any attention. When I'd gone undercover I'd kept my first name, but of course dropped my surname, Cleever, for the rather ironic one of Hunter. Back in Canberra I'd trained all my colleagues at the Australian Security Intelligence Organization to call me Denise, but I was fighting a losing battle here. Maybe it was the heat that led to the cropping of names.

In some cases it was an advantage, and Seb was an example. I wondered what his parents could have been thinking of when they named him Sebastian. I figure it's hard to look like a Sebastian at the best of times, for Seb it was impossible. He looked like a plain, single-syllable name like Ron or Sam, or maybe Joe. Bulging with muscles, he was built like a professional wrestler, but had the sunny, uncomplicated nature that I imagined went with a sweet-natured florist, or maybe a mild kindergarten teacher. He had short sandy hair, a flush of high color on his face, and a wide gap between his top front teeth. Seb was also bisexual, information he'd shared with me shortly after our first introduction.

He reached over me into the refrigerator and purloined a chicken leg from a plastic box clearly labeled JEN'S - DON'T TOUCH!!

"That's Jen's," I observed.

"She won't mind," he said through a mouthful. "We're an item."

Somehow I doubted that. Jen was a willowy redhead who had her sights set considerably higher than Seb. She'd been seen kissing Quint Aylmer, the youngest son, under a tropical moon, at least that's what Pete had told me during our shift this morning.

"So what's the gossip?" I said, settling for a can of Coke to keep me going while I decided what to eat. Seb had been at Aylmer Resort for at least a couple of years, which was more than most of the staff, so he was an excellent source.

He leaned against the nearest counter while he demolished the rest of the chicken leg. Waving the bone at me, he said, "Take your pick. I'm an authority on practically everything and everybody."

"What do you know about Roanna Aylmer?"

Seb pursed his lips. "I hear she likes girls," he said. He grinned knowingly at me. "Or maybe you've discovered that firsthand already."

"Not me. She marched in this morning while I was behind the bar and embarrassed a guest called Eddie Trebonus."

Seb's pleasant face darkened. "Trebonus? The guy's a total fuckwit."

"You know him?" I was surprised. There were

18

several hundred guests on the island at any one time, and I thought Eddie had only been there a few days.

Seb was still frowning. "I was up at the Big House cleaning the pool when this bloke comes out and starts bossing me around, like he owns the place." The hand without the chicken bone formed a meaty fist. "I came near as dammit to decking the bastard."

The Big House was the Aylmer family's private living area, and although I'd never seen it, I gathered it was even more luxurious than the best of the resort's guest accommodations.

"So what happened?"

My question brought a satisfied smile. "Mr. Aylmer Senior came out and told him to shut the hell up."

I blinked. "He told his own guest to shut up?"

Seb nodded. "In so many words. Treated Trebonus like he was a servant or something. I kept working, of course, but I couldn't help but laugh. Trebonus got red, then he went off without a word."

I was ready to ask more, but Kay's skinny body came rocketing into the kitchen. "Guess what! Something awful's happened. *Again.*" Her sharp nose twitched. She was clearly gratified to be the bearer of bad tidings.

Kay's hair seemed to be reflecting her pleasure, standing out from her skull like a miniature beige Afro. Yes, *beige.* That was probably why I couldn't stand the woman, a fact I disguised with difficulty.

"Are you coming?" she demanded. "A guest's got drowned. You should be down at the pier. It's pandemonium!"

19

CHAPTER THREE

As usual, Kay had exaggerated. There was no pandemonium by the white wooden dock jutting out into the aquamarine water, but rather a quiet desperation, as Sven, the lifeguard for the resort's main swimming pool, worked on an inert body. Maneuvering around the knot of spectators, my feet squeaking in the fine-grain coral sand, I managed to avoid Jen, who was doing her best to shoo spectators away. She was a startling figure, with her milk-white skin, flaming red hair, and vehement gestures, but her efforts were doomed. As always seemed to happen with disasters, a mysterious communication process had advised everyone in the vicinity that something dramatic was underway and people were coming from all directions.

Usually I avoid acting like a vulture at accidents, but the person I was playing, Denise Hunter, would be an enthusiastic spectator, so I pushed my way into the group until I could get a better view. The victim was a male, well-built and with a thick head of dark hair matching the thicket on his chest. A wedding ring glinted on his flaccid left hand, and as no one nearby was sobbing inconsolably, I winced at the thought that his wife could be relaxing somewhere else on the island, having no idea that her husband was, in all probability, dead.

"Let me through, I'm a doctor." A slight, self-important woman in a yellow bikini shoved her way to the front.

I looked sideways at the fleshy man beside me. He had a shaved head and wore a disapproving expression, wraparound dark glasses, a minuscule purple bathing costume, and a coat of glistening oil.

"What happened?" I asked.

He frowned at me, clearly not pleased to be questioned. "Scuba diving," he said in a strong American accent, that to my amateur ear sounded like one from New York. He added with authority, "Amateurs get into trouble all the time." He gave a grunt of disapproval. "Diving without a partner — the height of stupidity."

"Do you know his name?"

He shrugged. "No idea."

"Lloyd Snead," said a female voice. Another Yank, but with a lighter intonation. The name she'd given rang an immediate alarm bell. I swiveled my head to look up at her face. I'm quite tall, but this woman was basketball-player height. "Lloyd Snead," she repeated. "We sat at the same table at breakfast this morning. He was really quite charming."

She had on a black two-piece, exposing skin that had been tanned so often that it was like lightly-oiled brown leather. She was probably in her mid to late thirties, but her face was a network of fine wrinkles. She looked over my head to flash a toothy grin at the fleshy man, "I've seen you around. I'm Cynthia Urquhart."

She waited expectantly for a reply. After an awkward pause, he said with reluctance, "Fallon. Oscar Fallon."

"Oscar! Quite a name." She gave a girlish giggle.

Oscar managed not to roll his eyes, but I felt no such restriction.

Cynthia was off and running. "You can call me Cindy. All my friends do." Oblivious to his expression, which I thought indicated that he would rather be dragged over hot coals than call Cindy, Cindy, she went on, "I thought you knew poor Lloyd. You were talking to him in the dining room this morning when I came in."

"I didn't know him."

His flat denial apparently irritated Cindy. She squinted until a web of wrinkles fanned out from the corner of each eye. "I saw you two together." She glanced my way, as if for support. "I did, you know," she said to me.

Oscar pulled back his lips in an irritated grimace. "So, we were talking. Doesn't mean I know a thing about him."

He turned his head away from her, indicating the conversation was over. Cindy muttered, "Rude bastard," and moved off.

Oscar might not have known anything about Lloyd Snead, but I did. My preparation for this assignment had included intensive briefing of all the possible players I might come across on the island. Snead was a constant visitor, a banker who was rumored to be deeply into money laundering, but so far he'd evaded any specific charges. I inquired mildly, "Any idea who found Mr. Snead?"

Oscar gave a quick nod in the direction of a young boy, biting his lower lip, who stood back from the crowd. "That kid. He was swimming twenty meters off the beach when he started yelling for help. I went in and we dragged the guy out onto the sand. He was dead then, so it's a waste of time trying to revive him now."

It seemed he was right. The only movement in Snead's body was caused by Sven's unceasing efforts at resuscitation. The doctor put a hand on Sven's arm, and shook her head. A hush had fallen over the crowd, as it became clear that the man was dead.

When I made my way over to the kid I saw that he was shivering, even with the tropical sun heavy on his shoulders. "Hey, that must have been awful," I said, genuinely feeling the sympathy I was putting into my voice.

He looked at me, blank eyed. "Yeah, it was."

"So what happened?"

"Dunno." The boy gestured toward the mangroves that marked the end of the beach. "I was snorkeling over there, and I thought I saw a dolphin." He wiped a hand over his face. "But it was this guy, sort of hanging in the water. I thought he was alive, at first, because his arms were sort of waving." He swallowed. "But then he sort of rolled over, and I saw his face."

"Was he wearing scuba gear?"

The kid nodded. "Yeah, tanks and all that, but the mouthpiece was loose, just floating by his face."

"Do you know where the tanks are now?"

He frowned at me, as though at last he was wondering why I was asking all these questions. "The guy who helped me — we pulled the tanks off and left them on the sand."

I looked in the direction he was pointing, but the pale beach was bare of any scuba equipment. I opened my mouth to ask another question, but a deep masculine voice behind me said, "You the kid who found him? Yes? You'd better come with me."

I turned around to the handsome, petulant face of the younger Aylmer brother, Quint. He looked me up and down, read my name badge, and said, "Are you supposed to be on duty, Denise?"

"No. I'm between shifts."

Quint gave me an electric smile that lasted just long enough to show off his superior dental work. "Don't take this the wrong way, Denise, but it doesn't make a good impression to have staff hanging about. Get my drift?"

I got it, sending him a you're-the-boss look that brought an infuriatingly satisfied expression to his face. I was aware that Jen was hastening in our direction, so I sauntered off, not too fast, in case Quint Aylmer really thought I was rushing to obey him. I lurked in the palm trees until he and the kid left, then went back to check the beach for the scuba gear. It wasn't there.

Even if Snead survived, the Queensland cops would be called in to investigate the accident, so I knew that my boss at ASIO would be alerted that something had happened. I was deep undercover, so I couldn't risk a telephone call, even on a cellular phone, especially as we had information that the Aylmers had equipped the island with cutting-edge electronic surveillance apparatus. They also checked out staff exhaustively, and ASIO's work in establishing my identity had paid off there. Denise Hunter had a birth certificate, educational records and a string of jobs that suited an itinerant worker. Documentation showed she'd spent quite a lot of time traveling overseas, which made it simpler to fill in the gaps here in Australia.

I recalled my trainer saying, "You've got to believe you *are* this person, Denise Hunter, twenty-four hours a day. Maybe no one's observing you, but always act as if there's a video camera following you everywhere you go, even watching you while you sleep. Take it as a given that your things may be searched, so everything you have with you must fit the personality and lifestyle of the individual you now are. Never, ever step out of character, no matter what happens."

"So I can't pack my collection of leather-bound Jane Austin's?" I'd said. He'd rolled his eyes.

Together, we'd built up a personality and a history for Denise Hunter. She is a hard worker but is easily bored, so she doesn't last long at any job. A bit of a gossip, Denise loves travel, and is always out for a good time. Not into deep thought, she is basically pleasant, shallow and hedonistic.

"Not a bit like me," I had said to my trainer. He'd laughed.

Now I had to find out more about what had happened to Lloyd Snead without behaving in such a way as to call attention to myself. I wandered off to the dive shop and chatted up the cheerful young man who was in charge of outfitting guests with diving equipment. His yellow hibiscus shirt had the name tag TIM. I'd seen him around, but never spoken to him.

"One of your customers has pretty near drowned," I observed.

"Mr. Snead? Yeah, I heard."

"Bit of an amateur, was he?"

Tim shrugged. "Most of the guests are. I gave him an introductory lesson, and he seemed to get everything straight."

"Someone said he was diving alone."

He made a face at me. "If he'd listened to me, he'd have known that was a no-no."

I gave him a mischievous grin. "You didn't send him out with empty tanks, did you, Tim?"

"Not a chance," he said, mock indignant. "Anyway, Mr. Snead didn't get any tanks from me this morning."

"No? Then where would he have got them?"

"Search me. All I can say is he wasn't using any equipment from here."

I didn't imagine many guests came with their own tanks, as they were both bulky and heavy, so it was interesting to consider where Snead had got the ones he was wearing. It didn't seem wise to ask any more questions, so I said good bye to Tim and set off to get a late lunch.

Jen caught up to me as I walked up the hill to the staff accommodations. Her fair skin flushed hectic pink, rather an unfortunate contrast with her flaming red hair, she panted, "I saw you talking with Quint."

It was clear I was to reassure her that I wasn't impinging on her territory. "Mr. Aylmer told me to get lost, basically. He thinks staff members shouldn't mix with the guests on social occasions."

"Social —?" Jen broke off to punch me playfully. It hurt. Those skinny white arms of hers could deliver quite a blow. "You're so funny, Denise," she said. Her expression sobered. "The guy's dead, you know. All that work Sven did was for nothing, really, since the doctor said the guy'd drowned some time ago." She scrunched up her face. "I couldn't do that mouth-to-mouth thing, could you?"

"You kiss people," I said reasonably. "That's mouth-to-mouth."

"Yuck," said Jen, scrunching up her face even more. "You're sick. I wouldn't kiss a *dead* person."

Moving away in case she felt impelled to punch me again, I said, "Did you know the guy? I heard his name was Lloyd Snead."

"No." She stopped to consider. "The name's familiar. Maybe Quint mentioned him." She said Quint's name with emphasis. "Why do you want to know?"

"No particular reason." There was no point in asking her any more questions. Jen was single-minded, but she was also sharp. The last thing I wanted was her telling Quint Aylmer that I was interested in Snead's death. "You working tonight?" I asked.

This inquiry was guaranteed to get an enthusiastic response: Those who were on shift complained about the difficulties of their jobs, generally illustrating this with stories of past horrors; those not scheduled to work exulted in that fact, mentioning cheerfully what they intended to do with their freedom. Jen was of the latter group.

"I'm hoping to spend a little time with Quint, actually," she said with a sly smile. "Of course we can't be seen anywhere in *public*, because of him being an Aylmer and all, but that could change, if ..." She let her voice trail off as she shot me a meaningful look.

"So you're really serious, then? I thought you liked Seb."

"Seb?" Her tone was affectionately disparaging. "Seb's very nice, but ..." She flashed me a brilliant smile. "Hey, Denise, if *you* want him — I'm not keen on him any more."

"I'm not interested in Seb."

"No? Because you're gay? But surely you're bi?"

I didn't move quickly enough to avoid her playful biceps punch. "I mean," she said, "like, practically everybody is."

Friday night at the Tropical Heat Cocktail Lounge was only surpassed by Saturday night for noise, drunken guests and raucous behavior. I'd wondered why it made any difference what night it was in a holiday resort, until Pete had pointed out that some guests only came for the weekend, flying in or coming by launch from the mainland to arrive early Friday evening, departing in a crowd late on Sunday.

Besides Pete and me behind the bar, there were three other staff to serve the tables, including Kay of the startled beige hair. It had to be dyed — but I couldn't imagine anyone *choosing* that particular shade.

"Awful about the guy drowning," she said while she waited for me to fill a drink order. It was for eight beers, so I didn't have to concentrate.

I knew Kay had spent most of the afternoon in the main office of the admin building, filling in for someone who was off sick, so I said, "Did the cops come?"

Raising her voice, as the decibel level was already approaching the pain threshold, Kay said, "It was the same two who flew over last time. The young one is really cute. Sort of like a really young Mel Gibson, you know? Of course, they weren't much interested. I mean, this was just a drowning — the guy before had his head blown off."

When I'd first arrived at Aylmer Island I'd been given exhaustive descriptions of how grotesque the shooting death had been, and the note of regret in Kay's voice indicated how sorry she was that this later accident hadn't been up that standard. I said, "Pity Snead wasn't mauled by a shark, to make it worth the cops' time."

My tone had been a little too dry. Kay gave me a puzzled glance, then said, "There were reporters and everything last time. The place was buzzing. I saw myself on the telly — I didn't talk, or anything. I was just in the crowd."

It was fortunate that Lloyd Snead's death hadn't been deemed newsworthy. Television crews delighted in background shots to fill in the gaps. Should the media descend on Aylmer Resort there would always be the chance that my face would be beamed into Australia's living rooms, a less than desirable occurrence.

Apart from worries about the media, I lived in fear that I'd look up from the bar and see someone I knew heading my way. "Denise!" I could imagine him or her exclaiming. "What are you doing here? Resigned from ASIO, have you?"

I'd been undercover a few times, and nothing like that had ever happened to me, but I'd heard alarming tales from other agents about how their covers had been blown.

Kay swept her laden tray off the counter with an ease I had to admire as her slight frame seemed too delicate to lift anything of weight. "The guy's wife isn't too broken up," she said. "That's her in the lime green in the corner."

I followed her glance. Kay was right, the woman in the tight green dress seemed quite at ease, or as at ease as one could be when chatting to Eddie Trebonus. She was attractive in an overblown rose sort of way. Blondish hair, pink cheeks and a voluptuous body. I made a bet with myself that she did a Marilyn Monroe waltz with her hips when she walked. So much for my vision of a weeping, inconsolable widow.

To my chagrin Eddie had seen me looking in their direction. He grinned widely and raised a hand to wave. I repressed a shudder and hurried to join Pete as he labored to serve the voracious patrons lining the bar.

"Harvey Wallbanger," demanded another customer. I could do that cocktail easily, as it was a simple mixture of vodka and orange juice with Galliano dribbled on top. The ones I hated were the multi-ingredient drinks, where I had to rush around the back and check my trusty *Bartender's Guide* yet again. Even with that assistance I sometimes got confused, so there was a possibility I'd invented a new cocktail or two, not that most of the patrons would know on a busy night, where they were as intent on throwing down the alcohol as I was in clearing one order for the next.

"Red alert," said Pete ten minutes later. "Your nemesis is heading this way."

Eddie shoved his way into a gap at the crowded bar and grinned at me. It was a pity I couldn't feel even a twinge of gratitude at his obvious pleasure in my company, but at least I didn't recoil too obviously when he reached over to paw at me with thick fingers. "Busy tonight, Den?"

I took a step back. "It's Denise."

"Well, *Denise . . .*" Eddie paused to snicker at his use of my full name, then he went on with an aggravating smirk, "What I have in mind is a real test for you. I'm asking for a Ramos gin fizz. What do you say to that?"

Gin fizz I knew. Gin, sugar syrup, lime, lemon, soda water and a cherry, but what in hell were the ingredients of a Ramos gin fizz?

"I wouldn't have one of those particular fizzes," I said. "I've heard they're dangerous. A real health risk."

Eddie gazed at me, astonished, then a smile slid onto his fat lips. "You don't say."

Before he could go on, Pete came up. "I'll fix the order," he said. "Denise, you're wanted at the back door." He followed me as I moved away.

31

"Thanks," I said, appreciating how sweet he was to save me.

"No, I mean it," Pete said. "There's someone to see you. And for God's sake, hurry back." He gestured at the crowd pressing against the bar. "The barbarians are at the gate, and they're bloody thirsty."

The door was ajar, a breaking of the strict rule that it should always be kept closed and locked. I opened it fully and stepped through. "Denise," said Roanna Aylmer.

I have to admit my heart jumped and my blood fizzed rather like the cocktail that Pete was no doubt preparing for Eddie at that very moment. "Ms. Aylmer," I said, ever polite.

She made an amused sound, deep in her throat. "I think you can call me Roanna."

"Roanna," I said. It was an unfamiliar name to me, but it suited her dark good looks.

"I have a favor to ask."

Voice neutral, I said, "Oh yes?"

"I've already asked Pete, and he's agreed to be a bartender at a function my family's having tomorrow night up at the Big House. He needs an assistant, and I wonder if you'd join him there around seven."

Perfect, I thought, *but don't answer too fast.*

Roanna obviously took my silence for a possible refusal. Her forehead crinkled, convincing me she was surprised I hadn't jumped at the chance. After a long pause, she said, "I know it's your night off, but I'll arrange for you to receive extra pay."

"Okay." I was offhand.

She was still frowning. "Don't do it if you don't want to," she said, an astringent note in her voice.

My smile was moderate. "Tomorrow night's fine."

A light movement in the air brought the heavy smell of tropical flowers. I looked at her firm lips. *We could seal the bargain with a kiss*, I thought.

Roanna tilted her head, measuring me. I hoped she couldn't read my mind, which was skittering past a kiss to activities even more alluring. "Seven o'clock," she said. "It'll be an interesting night."

"You're telling me," I murmured to her retreating back.

CHAPTER FOUR

When I finally plodded up the hill to the staff quarters my feet were aching, my sinuses stinging from cigarette smoke, and my ears still ringing from the din. After the cocktail lounge had closed at three I'd stayed behind with Pete to tidy up the bar, and then he'd gone loping off for what he called an assignation. From his anticipatory smile, I gathered that his date was pretty crash hot, but he didn't volunteer a name, and I didn't ask.

The full moon had already set, so there was no competition for the milky way, which blazed in countless points of light. As I walked up the final incline I scanned for anything out of place. This was a habit encouraged by my training, but it was also because I was keenly aware that the route was ideal for an ambush. Lush vegetation crowded each side of the way. The only illumination was provided by a series of ankle-high lights positioned every few meters to throw fans of brilliance on the surface of the path itself. This was a great help as far as sure-footedness went, but of absolutely no use if someone was skulking in the undergrowth. There was no reason to suppose I was under any threat, but Lloyd Snead's death had unsettled me. It could have been an accident, but my instincts told me otherwise.

To cheer myself up, I fantasized Roanna Aylmer lurking in the bushes, a faint smile on her lips. She would step out onto the path and offer a casual invitation for a walk in the tropical night. I'd play hard to get, as I didn't want her to think I was a pushover. It was an enticing thought, but naturally she didn't appear, so, tired but not the slightest bit sleepy, I went to the rec room in search of a cup of coffee.

As usual, there were still people up and partying. I wandered, yawning, into the kitchen, where Seb was entertaining an attentive audience. His sandy hair standing on end and his face flushed with laughter and, judging by the beer in his hand, alcohol, he declared with drama, "So George Aylmer collects me and Ivy before he fronts the new widow. I'm there to pick Lainie Snead up off the floor if she faints." He grinned at Ivy Bestlove. "And Ivy's ready to minister smelling salts or whatever."

Ivy Bestlove was the imperturbable resort nurse

who was accustomed to ministering to coral scratches, sunburned skin and other mishaps that guests encountered. She was efficient, attractive in a cool way, and friendly, but reserved. Although I'd chatted to her several times, I was no closer to understanding what made her tick.

"What happened?" asked Kay, who was drinking some hideously colored health potion that she jealously guarded, as if any of us would even want to taste the stuff.

Seb hated to be hurried when he was telling a story. "I'm getting to it," he said, nettled. A couple of people lost interest and wandered away, so he started off again in a louder voice. "So the three of us go to find Lainie Snead to break it to her that her husband's been drowned. 'I'm afraid I've some very sad news,' George Aylmer says when we find her sunbaking on a lounge beside the hotel pool. You know what Lainie's response is?" Seb looked from face to face with an encouraging expression. "Is anyone going to guess?"

"Get on with it, Seb!" yelled Bruce. He had a hard, wiry body and a face made menacing by narrow, black eyes and a perpetual sneer. He was a heavy drinker, even by staff standards, and at this time of morning looked even more hungover than usual.

Irked, Seb frowned at him, then went on, "Lainie says, 'Spit it out, George,' like she doesn't think it's odd that the three of us have turned up at the poolside. George suggests that we all go inside where it's private, but she sits up and says, Just tell me, so he does."

Seb paused for effect, but a few muttered come on's got him going again. "There I am, poised to catch her if she swoons, and Ivy's ready to give first aid, or at the very least a comforting female arm..." Another pause.

"I'm going to bed," someone announced.

"So," said Seb, goaded into speeding up his narrative, "George Aylmer tells her that her husband's been drowned in a scuba diving accident and the cops are on their way from the mainland. As cool as you please, she asks for details, and then she says, `Your negligence, I suppose. I imagine I'll be suing the resort.' And then she gets up and walks off, leaving us standing there."

"Lainie Snead was in the Tropical Heat tonight," I volunteered, "wearing a green dress with cleavage and a half."

I've never liked gossiping, but Denise Hunter was the sort to enjoy it. Besides, it was the currency that got you gossip in return, and I was there to get as much information as I could about the Aylmers and everyone around them.

"Lainie Snead's always been a bit of a bitch," said Kay.

There were general sounds of agreement. "How come you all seem to know her?" I asked.

Several people chuckled. Seb said, "Everyone knows the Sneads. They've been coming to the resort every three months or so for the couple of years I've been here. He's some high executive in banking, and she's into spending whatever money he makes. In her spare time she complains about the staff."

"Remember the time she said Quint Aylmer made a pass at her?" said Kay. "I was in admin when she came storming through the door demanding to see Moreen Aylmer about her randy son." Laughing com-

ments indicated that the consensus was that Quint
was almost certainly guilty as charged.

Just as everyone started talking about other
things, Vera Otterlage said, "If you're female and
breathing, watch out!"

Vera's timing had fascinated me from our first
meeting. Petite, energetic, and with wide, bulging blue
eyes, she always got the joke too late — sometimes not
at all — or made a comment when the subject had
already changed. It was as if she was a beat or so
behind the music that everyone else heard.

Vera bounced on her toes, looking around brightly.
"Does Jen know about Quint Aylmer?" she asked. "I
mean, really, someone should warn her."

There was an odd undercurrent of dislike in the
room. "Why don't you do that, Vera?" said Ivy
Bestlove.

Apparently oblivious to the scorn in Ivy's voice,
Vera said, "Oh, I couldn't! I'm not really friends with
Jen ever since that day she punched me."

"In the mouth, I hope," said Bruce. Vera wasn't
popular, but Bruce had gone further than most, and
actively despised her.

Vera blinked at him. "On the arm, actually. I still
don't know why. I never did anything to upset her."

This brought derisive hoots. Vera stuck out her
bottom lip.

I said helpfully, "Jen must have misunderstood
something you said."

Vera nodded, partly mollified by my supportive
tone. "Jen's just impossible! You know how I'm always
trying to be a good friend, so I don't see why she's
picking on me."

Trying was the word for Vera. She was one of the

most irritating people I'd ever met, but as she was involved in the day-to-day organization of the various conventions and conferences Aylmer Resort hosted, I was cultivating her friendship, particularly since an important conference was coming up in a few days. Being friends with Vera was an uphill job — several times I'd been sorely tempted to hit her myself.

Convention facilitator was her title, and she mentioned it at every opportunity. It was surprising to me that Vera had such a responsible job, as it was hard to imagine her organizing anything that was in the slightest complicated. She'd been at the resort for over a year, however, handling the details of at least twenty-five events. This information Vera had imparted while we'd been having a tiresome heart-to-heart a couple of days earlier, a conversation that mainly consisted of me making sympathetic noises and Vera complaining how she wasn't really appreciated.

It was one of Vera's fetching idiosyncrasies that she pronounced *really* as *rilly*, a fact that led to much merriment at her expense, as people said things like, "Do you rilly, rilly believe that, Vera? Rilly truly?" Then went off guffawing, leaving her looking after them with a puzzled frown.

I sighed to myself. I wasn't up to cultivating friendship with Vera at nearly four o'clock in the morning, even if she was staring at me expectantly with her prominent blue eyes. I said, "I'm going to bed."

"Why can't people be nice?" Vera asked me. "I mean, it rilly isn't that hard to be pleasant, is it?"

"It rilly isn't," I agreed. Now *I* was doing it.

* * * * *

39

Exhausted, I opened my door and turned on the light. All the bedrooms had locks, but I never used a key when I was leaving. After all, I had nothing to hide, did I?

I shut the door behind me and followed my usual routine of looking around. Paranoid or not, I kept my expression casual, just in case my trainer had been right and there was a video camera watching me. When I'd first been assigned to this room I'd made a thorough search, and I was almost positive the only thing that might be concealed was some tiny listening device, though I thought even that was highly unlikely. Why should anyone suspect me of anything? And what would they hear, anyway? I hoped I didn't snore. Now that would be embarrassing.

Usually I went through a quick visual check then went on with what I was doing. This time I caught my breath. Someone had been there. There was a subtle difference in the arrangement of several key things. I'd been careful to place the novel I'd been reading so it was aligned with the edge of the desk. The book had been moved. Of course, it was possible that one of my workmates was captivated by Denise Hunter's choice of light entertainment, *Raw Embers of the Heart,* and had popped in to look at it. That thought evaporated when I noticed that the bedspread was no longer tucked exactly as I'd left it, nor was the beige plastic chair precisely as I'd positioned it.

A quick check of drawers confirmed that my room had been searched. Whoever it was had been careful, but there was no way he or she could replace every single item as I had left them. Whoever it was now knew that I took aspirin and wore contact lenses, that I used herbal shampoo and shaved my legs. In the top dresser drawer I kept some cheapish jewelry, a pencil flashlight, and a box of tissues. There were a couple of faked-up letters from friends, a note from my "mother," two postcards, one from Britain, the other Canada, ostensibly from friends I'd made overseas. There were also a few photos, most featuring me with family or at some social gathering with friends. No address book, no diary.

The middle drawer held my underclothes, and I cringed to think that someone had pawed through them. In a bottom drawer I had a passport with all the essential entry and exit stamps to show that Denise Hunter had traveled widely overseas. There was also a driver's license in her name, and two credit cards. Although there was an option for staff to put valuables in a safe, I wanted anyone who might search my things to have no difficulty finding material that confirmed my identity.

I had a little grin to myself, thinking of how I'd wondered whether the character I was playing would be bringing a selection of sex toys and explicit literature to the island. In the end I hadn't even included a multispeed vibrator to jazz up the overall image. Now I'd been searched, it seemed rather a pity I hadn't spiced up Denise's persona with startling equipment.

I sat on the edge of the bed to think about the situation. Maybe I'd triggered attention because of my questions about Lloyd Snead, though I didn't think I'd shown more than the normal curiosity about the accident. In fact, if I were being monitored, *not* to show at least some interest in the fact a guest had drowned just off the main beach of the resort would have been suspicious.

More worrying was the possibility that there was something wrong with my cover story, some inconsistency that had set off an alarm. There was a reason for the Aylmers to run stringent checks on staff, and it had nothing to do with normal business practices. ASIO had isolated a list of Aylmer activities that were potentially a threat to Australia's security, including the provision of new identities for international terrorists, who were provided with everything necessary to prove that they were legal Australian immigrants who had become citizens of their new country. In our multicultural society, they would have no trouble being accepted as genuine, and with Australian passports, they were free to travel the world undetected.

Since the Aylmers appeared to be expert in providing false identities, it had taken months of preparation to set up Denise Hunter's cover. It had to be much more detailed than usual so that even a close examination wouldn't expose me as a plant. It also meant that I had to be a clean plant: I couldn't carry any weapons or communications gear, I couldn't make contact through the usual channels of mail, telephone or satellite-link computer. I was on my own, and the only messages I could give or receive had to be person-to-person, using a level of caution that would be ludicrous in other circumstances.

It was only when I was cleaning my teeth in the echoing concrete of the ablutions block that another explanation for the search came to me. Roanna Aylmer. She'd shown some interest in me, fleeting perhaps, but still interest. Perhaps that was enough to make me an object of surveillance. I raised my eyebrows at my reflection in the mirror over the basin. If a couple of brief conversations was all it took to trigger this response, it seemed a pity not to not do something exciting with Roanna that would justify all the attention I was getting.

On my way back to bed I had another thought. What if *Roanna* had searched my room, or had someone search it for her? I had to smile at my conceit: There was no reason to believe that Roanna Aylmer was smitten with me. It was far more likely that she was bored, and I had provided a moment or two's entertainment.

If anyone was smitten, it was me. Well, *smitten* was rather too strong — perhaps *attracted* was a better word. Whatever, it was my job to gain as much information about the Aylmers as possible, so I'd have to find a way to encourage Roanna to get close to me. It was absolutely my duty.

CHAPTER FIVE

I woke with a slight headache and a dry mouth.
The cheap clock radio I'd brought to the island with
me announced the time to be eleven-ten. Lying on the
narrow metal-frame bed — deliberately chosen, perhaps, to discourage staff-to-staff couplings —I explored
the ceiling for a suspicious lens. There was nothing
but a spiderweb in one corner and a light brown
water stain the shape of Tasmania.

A trickle of sweat slid down the side of my face. It
was like lying in a beige shoebox filled with breathless
heat. I refused to use the air-conditioning unit in the

window because it operated with a near-deafening roar, relying instead on the rackety ceiling fan for some relief. Unfortunately, when the blades were slowly turning only the faintest draft of air brushed my skin. It wasn't an option to turn the fan to a higher setting, because each notch upward made it creak even more arthritically, and at full speed it vibrated with such alarming oscillations that it seemed ready to tear itself out of its mountings and scythe murderously through the room.

I gathered my things, put on a shorty dressing gown for decency, and padded out to the ablutions block to have a long shower and wash the smell of smoke out of my hair. Tonight was the Aylmer function where I would tend the bar and keep my ears and eyes on full alert. The rest of the day was mine, and I intended to spent it alone. After the sustained noise of the cocktail lounge last night, I craved the absence of human voices.

In denim shorts, a T-shirt that proclaimed WHATEVER THEY SAY, I FOLLOW THE VOICES IN MY HEAD, and hiking boots, I set out to conquer the most grueling of the several rain-forest trails marked on the map given to guests. So far I'd hiked several of the easier routes, but this one was marked as strenuous, going up to the highest point of the island and down the other side.

With a pleasant feeling of flouting the rules, I left off my name badge. We had all been told repeatedly that guests must recognize us as being "an Aylmer person" at all times, even when we weren't on duty. I didn't intend to meet anyone else, guest or not, so there was no reason for me to wear my name. In my backpack I had binoculars, water, fruit and a health bar that promised to provide all the energy needed for an active life. Of course I knew that it was highly unlikely anyone wished me harm, but I noted that the only thing I carried that could conceivably be a weapon was a combination knife, with blades, screwdriver, and a handy little tool that I vaguely thought was intended to get stones out of horses' hooves.

Soon I escaped the brassy sunlight for the cover of the rain-forest canopy. After the eye-squinting glare of the tropical sun, the light here was eerie, a kind of strangled green that had been filtered through many layers of vegetation. The heavy air was full of the pervasive smell of wet earth and rotting plant matter. Huge ferns sprang from the spongy ground, thick vines looped theatrically over branches as though they'd been deliberately strung there, and I could hear the faint trickling sound of running water. Immediately I thought of leeches, and hastened up the path away from the damper areas.

The incline became steeper, my thighs began to ache, and sweat stung my eyes. I stopped several times, not to rest, I assured myself, but to admire the rain forest. I'd read up on the ecosystem and was pleased with myself when I identified wild orchids, Bangalow palms with their odd, finger-like air roots, the vicious thorns of monkey puzzle vines, and, most disconcerting of all, I thought, giant strangling figs whose lethal embrace was slowly throttling their host trees.

An hour into the climb — it had ceased to be a walk — I was panting, my T-shirt was sticking to me, and my backpack was growing heavier with every step.

If I wanted to be alone, I'd chosen the perfect excursion. I couldn't imagine anyone else hardy enough, or stupid enough, to slog up this path in such steamy heat.

The final meters of the minimountain were bare rock. Blinking, I came out into brilliant sunshine. The view burst upon me like a shout. I was at the highest point of the island, and an exhilarating glow of achievement filled me. In front of my feet the ground fell away precipitously, plummeting hundreds of meters to the pale green of the golf course and the toy buildings of the hotel, the convention center and the administration offices. All this was edged with a margin of white sandy beaches, and then the turquoise shadings of the shallow sea. To the north, a string of tiny uninhabited baby islands, looking impossibly beautiful, seemed to float like a green necklace in the sparkling water.

"Hello," said a voice behind me.

I literally jumped. "Hell!"

"Sorry. Did I startle you? Denise, isn't it? From the bar?" Biddy Gallagher grinned at me, hands on hips, knowing full well that my heart had done an alarmed somersault in my chest.

Angry because I'd been taken by surprise, and keenly aware that if Biddy had meant me harm, I could have been pitching over the cliff without having any idea what was happening, I snapped, "And where were you lurking?"

"Lurking? I came up the other way, and reached the top a moment after you." She seemed not to feel the heat: Her long face was dry, her khaki shirt crisp, her shorts still immaculate. Her grin widened as I moved away from the edge of the cliff. "Afraid of heights?"

"You might take a fancy to blip me over." With an effort, I'd achieved a light tone.

Biddy cackled. "What? My novel way of complaining about slow service in the Tropical Heat Cocktail Lounge?"

Still irritated, I shrugged off my backpack and opened it. "Fruit? A drink?"

We sat in the shade on a rocky outcrop at the edge of the vegetation. Biddy took a banana and peeled it neatly, so that the shaft rose out of yellow petals of skin. "I don't suppose you've got anything hard to drink?"

"Water only."

Biddy snapped off the top of her banana with large white teeth. She chewed ruminatively, then waved the stump at me and said, "A bit like eating a penis, don't you think?"

There was no way this woman was going to disconcert me. "I wouldn't know," I said primly. "My mother warned me not to do that sort of thing."

Biddy's chuckle made me smile too. "A fast mouth," she said, "I like that."

Selecting an appropriate blade on my combination knife, I sliced the top off a passionfruit and sucked out the sweet seeds inside. "Have you been to the resort before?" I asked, more for something to say than for any desire to hear the answer.

"No. And I don't expect to again."

"You don't like it here?"

Biddy raised a shoulder. "It's okay. A bit too glossy for my taste. Too much luxury makes me uncomfortable." She gave me a measuring glance. "And what about you? You don't strike me as the sort to work behind a bar."

"I don't?" I wasn't pleased to hear this, as I'd been congratulating myself that I had been doing pretty well in my role.

Biddy was clearly amused at my reaction. "Don't get me wrong," she said. "You do a great job, as long as Eddie Trebonus doesn't give you an exotic order that sends you around the back of the bar. Checking the ingredients, I imagine."

"Maybe."

"I get the impression you're slumming, if you know what I mean."

This was dangerous. If Biddy thought this, it was possible others did too. I said, sincerity to the fore, "This is the kind of life I like. Hate being tied down, you know? I've been all over the world, never settle any one place for very long."

"Uh-huh." Her tone was neutral.

"How about you?" I said, making a mental note to ask for a background check on her.

"I'm retired."

"I'll be rude," I said, "and ask. Retired from what?"

Biddy considered me for a moment, as though assessing what answer to give. Finally she said, "I was a cop."

An hour later, I was no wiser about Biddy Gallagher. We'd come down the path together, chatting, but she had been trying to pump me, and I'd been trying to pump her. The result was stalemate. Maybe it was the cop in her, but I couldn't help feeling that she was asking more questions than would be expected. There was no reason, I thought modestly, apart from my sparkling personality, for Biddy to pay much attention to me, but she showed the keenest interest in my activities. She also asked questions about other staff members, particularly the nurse, Ivy Bestlove.

I was intrigued when she asked me if I'd been on the island when the skeet-shooting accident had occurred. The victim, Morrie Bellamy, had worked for Abscound Electronics, a firm with sensitive defense contracts. It had been kept from the media, but just before his death Bellamy had contacted the federal cops with accusations of security breaches at his company. Before he could provide concrete details, he'd attended the convention on Aylmer Island where the accident had occurred. A covert investigation of Abscound was underway, and one of my tasks was to find out if the Aylmers had any involvement in Bellamy's death.

"The accident happened before my time," I said. "Why? Did you know the guy?"

"No," she said, a little too quickly. When I continued to look at her inquiringly, she added, "The resort's run so well, it's hard to imagine how something like that could happen."

With the air of one pronouncing a self-evident truth, I said righteously, "Where there's a loaded gun, there's always a chance of an accident."

She gave me a narrow look. "Have you ever fired a gun?"

I'd not anticipated Denise Hunter being asked this

question. I was an excellent shot with a range of firearms, but this certainly wouldn't be in Denise Hunter's experience. "I hate guns," I said, repressing an impulse to embroider my words with a realistic shudder.

It was always wise, my trainer had pointed out, to underplay, if possible. "That particularly applies to you, Denise," he'd said.

Biddy was tenacious. "So you've never fired a shotgun?"

The path had flattened out, and we were coming out from the rain-forest cover into the full glare of the sunlight near the island's nine-hole golf course. I fished around for my sunglasses. "I told you, I don't like guns." Using my best cheeky grin, I asked, "Why the third degree? Do you think it was me who blew the guy's head off?"

Watching me closely, Biddy said, "Not at all. It was a woman named Aileen Fountain."

"Was it?" I continued my expression of polite interest. Biddy had certainly done her homework. Aileen Fountain was indeed the name. She'd booked accommodation for the weekend, flown in from Brisbane on a Friday night, and killed Morrie the next morning. At the time it appeared to be nothing more than a dreadful mishap, but after giving evidence at the inquest, which found Morrie Bellamy's death accidental, Aileen Fountain had disappeared off the face of the earth. She had claimed to be a New Zealander, but later checking of her records showed that a person of that name had died before her first birthday.

"How come you know her name?" I said.

"I don't know, it just caught my eye."

51

Now, *I* would have thought of a much better explanation for remembering. I mused on it for a moment. Maybe I'd say that my best friend at school was an Aileen, or perhaps that *Fountain* had stayed in my mind because the word reminded me of the way blood must have spurted when the pellets shattered the victim's skull. Of course, this was the very thing my trainer had warned me about. "Keep it simple," he would snarl. "The more complicated you make it, the easier it is to trip you up, and the more it sounds like a fake story."

I said to Biddy, "And now there's been another awful accident." I shook my head in a where-will-it-end sort of way. "Did you run into Mr. Snead at the hotel?"

"I knew him by sight. Talked with his wife a couple of times."

In my gossipy persona, I said blithely, "I hear the widow isn't exactly shattered by grief."

Biddy's face hardened. "You'd know, would you?"

"That's what everyone says," I said, on the defense.

She grunted, clearly dismissing me as unfeeling. Watching her stalk off along the path to the hotel, I had a ridiculous impulse to run after her and explain, "Look, that was Denise Hunter speaking, not *me*."

When I got back to the staff buildings, George Aylmer was making one of his surprise inspections. He'd done one the very first day I'd been there, and I'd been warned to expect them at odd times in the future. "Everything satisfactory? Everyone happy?" he was asking Pete and a couple of others as I came in the front entrance.

The senior Aylmer was tall, but slightly stooped, holding his head as though he was expecting to walk through a low doorway at any moment. His thinning hair was streaked with gray, he had a hook nose, a firm mouth over a jutting chin, but his manner didn't quite match his commanding looks, being an odd combination of bossiness and hesitation.

Turning to me, he frowned as his glance swept across my breast. For a moment I thought it was the message on my T-shirt, but then I realized it was, horrors, my lack of a hibiscus badge reading *Denise*.

"Your tag!" he said.

"Left it in my room," I said, trusting that he would assume this dereliction of duty had just occurred.

"You know the rules."

"I'm sorry, Mr. Aylmer. I'll do better next time." I kept a straight face with difficulty, as Pete was making faces at me from behind George Aylmer's back.

My employer nodded, apparently pleased that I had immediately acknowledged my error. "At all times," he said, "our valued guests must know that they are surrounded by friendly Aylmer staff."

I could think of quite a few times the valued guests wouldn't be happy to have friendly staff breathing down their necks, but I contented myself with slanting my eyebrows the wrong way to indicate that I was regretful for my transgression.

George Aylmer waffled on for a few more minutes, then went off to annoy people in the rec room. I thanked Pete for trying to make me laugh inappropriately, and headed for my room. I was waylaid by Jen before I could reach its sanctuary.

"Den, you're going tonight, aren't you?" When I didn't immediately respond, she added with asperity, "To the party at the Big House. The Aylmers' place."

"I'm on the bar with Pete."

Jen wriggled her shoulders importantly. "I'd have been there, helping out too, but Quint asked me not to."

"Oh?"

"Quint says he couldn't stand to see me, like, serving people and all that. Not when I'm so important to him." She drew me aside, looking around as if she was about to impart a state secret. "The fact is," she said, "I wonder if you'd keep an eye out."

"For what?"

Jen's white skin flushed an unbecoming blotchy pink. "It's a bit embarrassing, but I know I can rely on you, Den."

"You can," I said.

"It's silly, I suppose, but Quint's mentioned this Cindy someone. She's one of the guests. I know he wouldn't be interested in her, but I get the feeling she's got ideas about him."

"Has he got ideas about her? I'd say that was the vital thing."

A heavy frown descended on Jen's face. "He says he hasn't, but *men*. You know what they're like."

"They just can't help themselves," I said helpfully.

She took my arm, a sister in suffering. "Exactly," she said. "So I want you to keep an eye out for me."

"You can have both of them," I said. "I'll report back tomorrow, okay?"

"Can this be our secret? I wouldn't like anyone to think I didn't trust him."

I made a zipping motion across my mouth. "Silent as the grave," I said.

It seemed there was a conspiracy to stop me from getting out of my sweaty clothes. Seb's bulky form stopped me in the corridor to my room. "Got a mo, Den?"

I sighed. "What?"

"I hear Roanna Aylmer has her eye on you."

Jeez, it was eyes everywhere. Not bothering to hide my exasperation, I said, "I've had two conversations with her, both of them short."

He patted my arm. "Just a word of warning," he said. "Her brother, Harry, is a bit protective."

This was getting past a joke. "Just what are you telling me?"

"None of Ro's friendships last very long. I wouldn't like you to get hurt."

"Oh, spare me! What are you, my big brother?"

Seb grinned and put one massive arm around my shoulders and gave me a substantial squeeze. "I'd love to be more than that, but you turned me down, remember?"

"So what's with Harry?"

"He'll know you and his sister have been talking."

"Creepy!"

Seb sucked his lips in and nodded sagely. "It is, a bit. What you should know is that she won't stay interested for long, and then you'll find your job's gone, and you'll be asked to move on."

"I'll be fired?" After all the trouble taken to establish me at the resort, this was not what I wanted to hear.

He spread his hands. "All I'm saying is that Ro

Aylmer's romantic interests don't hang around when the party's over. They either quit or they get the old heave-ho."

A bubble of anger filled my chest. "Thanks for the warning," I said, hearing the sudden coldness in my voice.

"You're not going to pay any attention, are you?"

"Look," I snapped. "I've hardly spoken to the bloody woman, so I've no idea why you've got it into your head that there's anything going on."

Seb's blunt-featured face was hurt. "Hey, I was only trying to help."

"Thanks, but that's help I can do without."

I could feel my cheeks burning with barely controlled rage. I took a deep breath, aware that this was quite an overreaction. I wondered why, until I abruptly realized that Seb reminded me of my sanctimonious elder brother, Martin, who had spent a great deal of my youth laying down the law for me, telling me what to do and whom to see.

"Sorry," I said. "I know you mean it for the best."

Seb bobbed his heavy head and left, still wounded. I dropped my pack in my bedroom and went to look for Pete, finding him slumped in front of the television in the rec room, a can of beer in one hand and a fat ham sandwich in the other. "You still haven't got your tag on, you naughty girl," he observed.

I flung myself into the chair next to him. "Seb's just taken upon himself to lecture me about friendship with Roanna Aylmer," I said. "He says her brother Harry is a problem."

Pete took a long swallow of beer. "Seb's obsessive about Harry. He's got a crush on him."

"Seb's got a crush on Harry Aylmer?"

The incredulity in my voice amused Pete mightily. "No accounting for taste, is there? Don't ask me why, but Seb's always gone for the brooding, risky sort, male or female."

"And what does Harry think of this? Is he gay?"

"Oh yes, he's gay, but I don't reckon Seb has a chance." Pete made a face at me. "Runs in the family. Wouldn't be surprised if Moreen turned out to be a closest lesbian."

The matriarch of the Aylmer clan a lesbian? He had to be pulling my leg. "You're kidding me, aren't you?"

"Maybe," he said with an aggravating smile. "But you should know that she's the power in the outfit. George Aylmer is the nominal head of the company, but basically his wife runs the whole show. She says jump, they ask how high."

"For God's sake, Roanna's an adult, and so, more or less, are her brothers."

"Sure. But the money and the authority are with Mum, and she doesn't let them forget it. That's half the trouble with Ro. She bucks, but she can't break away."

Reminding myself that I wasn't there to have a personal interest in Roanna, but a professional interest in the whole family, I said, "Who'll take over the running of the company eventually?"

Pete laughed. "Harry thinks it's going to be him, but it'll never happen. I'd reckon Moreen will hang on to the bitter end, and she looks to me like she's got a few decades in her yet." He took a huge bite of his ham sandwich.

"You know a lot about them."

He chewed, swallowed, and washed the food down

with another long draft from the can. "It's being a bartender," he said. "People tell you everything." He gave me a sly smile. "But you'd know that, being a bartender yourself."

"I lied."

"Did you, indeed?" His smile was speculative.

I nodded. "Yes," I said. "I'm not what I appear."

He sat up, all attention. "And what are you about to reveal to Uncle Pete?"

"That I'm a total fake," I said.

CHAPTER SIX

Pete and I walked up the rise to the Aylmers' sumptuous residence through scented air and the lazy rustle of coconut palm fronds. We both wore our working clothes of white shorts, canvas sneakers without socks, and the obligatory hibiscus shirt, mine red, Pete's a toxic yellow. And, of course, we each had our name tags displayed upon our respective chests.

At the security gate we were eyeballed by Bruce, who was on guard duty. With a rare flash of humor, he announced that we looked suspicious, but he'd let us through anyway. His usual sneer had been replaced by a thin-lipped smile, which was surprising enough for me to look back at him after we passed through the gate. Bruce raised a hand in a sort of awkward wave.

"I think Bruce likes you," said Pete.

"Oh, please, God, no!"

"It's the lure of the unattainable," said Pete. "It makes you irresistible."

I wasn't in a charitable mood. "Bruce is a thug and a drunk."

"He's got feelings, like everybody else." Pete chuckled at my expression. "Shall I tell him you're flying under false colors?"

Mock-indignant, I glared at him. "I might have been a little creative when I claimed on my job application to have had bartending experience, but I told you that personal detail in strict confidence."

He snorted. "You said, as I recall, that you were a total fake."

"I exaggerated. It's not a crime."

"If you lie about one thing," Pete pontificated, "you might well lie about another."

If you only knew. "I'm learning the bar stuff fast," I declared, "so my job application is getting truer all the time."

It wasn't dark yet, but tall flaming torches lined the pathway, creating an exotic, mysterious atmosphere, as though we'd been transported to the South Pacific of the sailing ships. My mind skittered away to think of cannibals, and, with my usual talent for irrelevancies, I remembered that human flesh was called *long pig* by the natives because it tasted rather like pork.

I was about to share this fascinating fact with Pete when he said, "You haven't been to the Big House before, have you? It's quite something."

It was. Surrounded by beautiful gardens, the main building was bounded on three sides by wide verandas of polished wood. The house itself was built around a large central courtyard, in the middle of which a striking fountain played, the water flowing over polished metal dolphins to splash into a pond crowded with fat koi fish. I knew that koi were impossibly expensive, but they still looked like overgrown goldfish to me. A light breeze of warm, fragrant air flickered the flames of the torches in the courtyard, giving an odd, wavering life to luxuriant ferns that were also illuminated by concealed lighting.

"George and Moreen live here in the main house," said Pete. "Their personal staff live in an adjoining building, but Roanna and her brothers each have an entirely separate little bungalow. Roanna's is the farthest away, and closest to the water."

A picture formed in my mind of a small house, hidden by lush tropical vegetation. It would have a veranda where one could sit, cool drink in hand, watching the light fade and the stars come out. "You've been there, Pete?"

He laughed. "No such luck. She's very picky who she takes home."

We were directed to a large woman with a pensive expression, who turned out to be the head of security for the Aylmers' private compound. She asked who we were, looked us over narrowly, and ticked our names off on a clipboard. "Please don't try to enter any of the private areas not opened for the function," she said. "If you do, an alarm will sound."

"She's new," said Pete as we walked away. "Otherwise she would have known me by name."

"Oh sure," I mocked. "You're practically a household word."

The level of protection was interesting. "Why do they need so much security for the Big House?" I asked.

"There are a lot of original artworks. At least, that's what I've been told."

"You're a friend of the family, and you haven't seen these artworks?"

"I'm Ro's friend. It's not the same thing."

All around us the activity was increasing as everything was set up. The Aylmers had their own house-staff working, of course, but functions of this size needed extra help, so apart from us there were several people I recognized from the resort.

Clusters of teak chairs around central tables formed islands where later guests could gather to eat and drink. Long trestles already held mouth-watering displays of food — mountains of prawns, whole lobsters, oysters nestling in pearly shells, salads galore. I'd skipped dinner, so I looked longingly in that direction. "Come on," said Pete, "you can eat later. Right now we've got to get everything ready."

Plates of appetizers were being distributed to the tables. To keep me going I snaffled asparagus rolls, miniature shish kebabs, and several chicken puffs.

The bar wasn't some temporary arrangement, but a fixture situated on the far side of the courtyard. It had sinks, running water, racks full of clean glasses, and a refrigerator and glass-washer under the counter. "Won't be too hard," said Pete, handing me a snowy apron mercifully free of hibiscus decorations. "Mostly it'll be wine, beer and standard stuff like rum and Coke, whiskey and soda, vodka and tonic. A few people might ask for Bloody Marys. Nothing complicated at all."

"Tell that to Eddie Trebonus," I muttered. Naturally I hadn't brought my trusty bar book, so if Eddie turned up, and I was sure he would, he'd just have to settle for something straightforward for a change.

"Watch out," said Pete, "the Dark Brothers are coming over."

The designation *dark* was fitting for Harry and Quint Aylmer. It was not only that they both had thick, black hair, deep brown eyes and heavily tanned skin. There was also a threatening atmosphere about them, enhanced by their broad-shouldered swagger and their identical, arrogant expressions. There was, however, a spark of intelligence on Harry's face: Quint merely looked sulky and rather dumb. I tried to visualize him from Jen's point of view. She was obviously enamored, but, try though I might, I couldn't see why. And what in hell would they talk about? Maybe they didn't talk. Maybe it was a strictly physical relationship. I repressed a gurgle of disgust at the vision that presented, busying myself with polishing a glass, another trick movie bartenders had taught me.

Harry leaned over the bar to inspect things. "You all set up?" he said to Pete.

Pete responded with a professional smile. "Ready to go."

Quint came behind to help himself to a Scotch. He

looked at me with disfavor. "You were on the beach when they dragged Snead out of the water." His tone made it sound as if I had deliberately flouted some you-must-not-be-on-the-beach rule. There didn't seem any sensible response, so I said nothing.

Quint turned to his brother. "Staff have to be told to keep out of the guests' areas at all times, unless they're there to work."

"You'll have to ask Dad about that."

Quint scowled. "Why? We're in charge of the day-to-day running of the resort, aren't we?"

Harry shrugged. "We can talk about it later."

Quint glowered at his elder brother's retreating back, then swung around to bark at us, "You keep everyone happy. Right? And no slacking. I want to see you hard at it, all the time."

As he stalked off, Pete said to me, "Don't let him get to you. He's kept on a short leash, and Quint doesn't like it. The trouble is that our Quint's not the brightest boy on the block, so no one's about to give him much responsibility, even his doting mother."

Stacking glasses neatly, I said, "How come you know so much about the Aylmers? And don't tell me it's because you're behind a bar."

"Me and Seb, we've been at the resort for the best part of three years. If you work in a place long enough, you find things out. And, of course, there's Roanna. We're good mates, and she often lets slip things about the family."

"Good mates?"

Pete chuckled. "Friends only. She gets lonely at times, and she comes down to the lounge for a chat, or meets me when I'm free and we go sailing or whatever."

"I thought there was a rule about staff socializing with management."

"No one's said anything to me."

That Roanna might be lonely was a new thought. She seemed cool and self-sufficient, but if she wanted a friend, I was available. Hell, I wouldn't mind being more than a friend. "Does she have much to do with the business?"

"Roanna, you mean? She set up the whole computer side of things — the Web page and online bookings, all that stuff." He made a face at me. "I don't understand any of it, but then, there'll never be a computer serving behind a bar, so it doesn't worry me."

The first people were arriving, and an unerring herd instinct for alcohol sent many our way. In a few moments we had gone from fiddling behind the bar to pushing past each other in our efforts to feed the voracious thirsts of guests. Most requests, as Pete had predicted, were for wine and beer, with an occasional mixed drink. The level of conversation in the courtyard became a buzz, and that, combined with the clatter of plates and silverware, almost drowned out the chuckle of the fountain and the soft mood music pouring out of little hidden speakers, one of which I'd almost squashed with a crate of soda water.

The gathering was a real United Nations affair. Most people spoke in English, sometimes heavily accented, but I overheard several other languages, two of which I understood. I spoke Japanese reasonably well, so I listened with attention to the conversation between two Japanese businessmen. Unfortunately it turned out to be an extremely dull deliberation about management problems in their respective companies.

The second conversation, in Indonesian, was much more interesting. Secure that no one in the company could understand them, a man and a woman discussed plans to bring illegal immigrants into Australia by way of a fleet of fishing vessels, landing their paying customers on a remote part of Australia's northern coastline, where they would be collected by all-terrain vehicles belonging to an ecotourism company. It was impossible to hear all the details, especially as I had to continue serving customers whilst not appearing to listen, but I gleaned enough to make it likely this particular shipment of human cargo would be intercepted.

They moved away, and I crouched down, ostensibly to collect clean glasses, but actually to close my eyes while I concentrated on committing to memory everything specific I'd heard.

"Are you hiding from Eddie?" Pete inquired.

I straightened. "You don't see him, do you?"

Pete was amused. "Not yet, but you'll entice him, I guarantee it." He snickered happily. "First Eddie, and then Bruce. Moths to a flame, both of them."

After the first onslaught, the demand had ebbed and flowed, and I found that our station behind the bar was a perfect place to observe what was happening from a position of near-invisibility. I was always amazed at how people treated servers of any kind as being, somehow, not there at all, even when discussing the most sensitive information without the apparent protection of a foreign language. From snatches of conversation I caught details of the latest scandal in television circles, some tips about Internet stocks, the name of the famous politician who was into whips and bondage, the aging star who was ditching his present wife for a teenage model, plus numerous references to things that without context made no sense at all but were pleasantly puzzling.

I scanned the crowd for Eddie Trebonus, but he didn't seem to be among the guests. I saw George Aylmer circulating, cigar in hand, spending a few moments with each group of people. Near the central fountain Quint Aylmer was looking terminally bored while Cindy from the beach towered over him, telling some story that caused her to gesture wildly and at intervals dissolve in gales of laughter. He didn't seem to be the type to stick around because it was polite, so I figured he had been told to entertain her.

Lainie Lloyd was there alone, wearing black and pearls. She was smoking a long brown cigarette in an even longer jeweled holder, so that for anyone closer to her than a meter, she posed a distinct eyeball threat. A little unsteadily, she came toward us. "White wine," she said. "Please."

As I handed her the glass, I looked into her face and saw misery and pain. Seb had been wrong. This woman wasn't nonchalant about her husband's death. And there was more than grief: I sensed fear and desperation.

Without thinking, I stepped out of my bartender role. "Can I do anything for you?"

It must have been the sympathy in my voice that made Lainie Lloyd look at me with such surprise. "Thank you, but no . . ." She set her shoulders. "I'm quite all right."

"Lainie." Harry Aylmer had appeared beside her. He glanced at me, then took her elbow. "Come and sit down."

She shook off his hand. "Thanks, but I'd rather be alone."

He moved away, but then stood still, watching her. Several people chose that moment to descend on the bar. As I took orders for drinks I was aware that she was staring at me, perhaps puzzled that a staff member would speak to her in such a personal tone. I looked for her a few minutes later when the surge of demand had abated, but she'd moved away.

My attention was riveted by Roanna, who was with a tall black man who was bending his head to listen to her, then replying in a deep velvet voice. Leaving Pete to serve, I gravitated to the end of the bar closer to them. They were too far away for me to make out what he was saying, but his tone made it sound important. Roanna gave him polite attention. She was wearing a short black dress, undeniably expensive, and high-heeled pumps. A single heavy gold band circled her throat, and she wore a gold watch. No other jewelry. I assured myself that this close observation was part of my job, but actually I was thinking what a stunningly attractive woman she was and how delighted I was that it was up to me to get close to her. I'd been plotting my strategies, and had decided being intriguing might capture her attention, but not *too* intriguing. I didn't want Roanna to think I had anything significant to hide.

In some way the weight of my glance seemed to impinge on Roanna, and she turned her head to look at me, an enigmatic expression on her face. I maintained a neutral expression until my view was blocked by a bumptious guy with a jutting jaw and hair cut so short it looked like a five o'clock shadow on his skull. He'd been in the cocktail lounge last night, loud, obnoxious and, by the end of the night, very drunk. He hadn't come up to the bar, so didn't remember me, but he'd made life miserable for Kate, who'd been serving his table, as well as any other female he and his Neanderthal mates had spied within sniggering distance.

His disposition didn't seem to have improved. "Hey, you, a beer," he demanded, jabbing his forefinger at me while he shouldered some inoffensive guy out of the way. He added with heavy sarcasm, "If it's not too much trouble."

I flashed him a smile edged with insincerity. "No trouble at all, sir."

He looked at me suspiciously, then glanced at my chest. "Denise, eh? You're new."

"I *am* new." My enthusiasm was totally feigned, but I was starting to have fun. "And I count it a privilege to work here at Aylmer Resort." I slapped a beer on the counter in front of him.

There was a low laugh. "Ah," said Roanna, who had moved closer to the bar, and obviously had heard my comment, "if only we had more employees like Denise." Her tone could hardly be more dry.

"Hello, Ro," he said. His intimidating manner had abruptly changed, and he wore an ingratiating smile.

"Go away, Tony."

He hesitated, obviously deflated, then picked up his beer, saluted her with it and, following her order, went away.

"Wow," I said. "Would you teach me to do that?"

"It requires a certain steel in one's character," said Roanna. "Would you have that?"

"Jeez," I said, "I'm afraid not. I'm a total pushover. Always have been."

Roanna did her raised-eyebrow trick. "Somehow I doubt that."

"Roanna." A command. From the introductory video I recognized Moreen Aylmer.

Roanna turned to her mother. "Yes?" Her tone was cool.

"You're neglecting our guests. I expect you to circulate, find people who seem left out, and introduce them to someone with whom they can chat. You know what to do."

Moreen Aylmer was formidable, as I'd heard her described by several people. She wore a severely tailored dark wine dress, diamonds studs in her ears, and a substantial diamond on her left hand. Solidly built, she had smooth dark hair, hawk eyes, and a stance that came from the habitual use of power. It was clear that she was accustomed to having her instructions obeyed without question.

After watching her daughter move away, Moreen Aylmer gave me a curiously assessing look. "Denise Hunter, isn't it?"

I nodded, murmuring assent in a suitably subservient manner. *Denise* was on my name tag, but it was surprising that the woman knew my full name. Why would she? I was just one of many working at the resort. I was rapidly becoming convinced it was because Roanna had paid attention to me, and I was willing to bet that the search of my room was just the beginning and that my personnel file had now been thoroughly checked.

Roanna's mother was still regarding me, so I remained demure. She said, "Are you enjoying it here at Aylmer Island?"

"Yes, of course."

She smiled wryly, suddenly looking very like her daughter. "Indeed? And what particularly do you enjoy?"

I had my answer ready. "I've always loved this part of the world. It's so beautiful."

There. Nothing to offend, and I'd neatly avoided any comment on the resort itself. If Roanna was going to be my way to get in close with the whole setup, I certainly didn't want to make an unfavorable impression on her redoubtable mother.

Moreen Aylmer nodded once at me, though whether in approval or dismissal I couldn't say, and swept away to hostess elsewhere.

"Mother Aylmer won't mind you eyeing Roanna," said Pete, laughing, "but just watch out if you pay attention to her precious Quint."

"Jen's in trouble, then."

He nodded. "She is, if Mama A finds out. And she will."

I tossed with Pete, and he won, so he left me in charge while he went to help himself unobtrusively to a plate of food, then go to the kitchen to eat it.

Standing behind the bar, I felt rather like the captain of a ship. The *SS Boozer*, perhaps. Or maybe the *Inebriation Express*. I was smiling to myself when I realized someone had spoken to me.

"Pardon?"

"I asked for Scotch on the rocks." The flickering light from the nearest flaming torch danced on Oscar Fallon's smooth, hairless skull. He looked at me more closely. "Didn't I see you on the beach?"

I nodded. "You'd just pulled Mr. Snead out of the water," I was going for a tone of admiration, and it seemed to work, as he threw his shoulders back, hero style. He was wearing a lightweight cream suit and a blue silk open-necked shirt, a considerable improvement on the tight purple bathers I'd last seen him in.

He said, "It was nothing. Anyone would have done the same."

I said smoothly, "Your choice of Scotch, sir? Johnny Walker? We have Black Label."

"Got Haig?"

"Of course." Haig Scotch was Biddy Gallagher's drink. I looked over Oscar's shoulder, wondering if she were there. As if summoned by my interest, she materialized on the other side of the courtyard and began to drift our way. "It was awful about Mr. Snead," I said to Oscar Fallon, sliding his drink in front of him. "I suppose the cops interviewed you, and everything."

He took a sip of his drink, and grunted his approval. "The cops?" he said. "I suppose they've got to do their job, but the whole thing was a total drag."

Although I murmured sympathetically, I was thinking that it was rather more a drag for Lloyd Snead, not to mention his wife.

"Thing is," said Oscar, "no one will know for sure what killed the guy until there's an autopsy, so asking me all those questions was a waste of time."

"I thought Mr. Snead drowned." I widened my eyes. "Are you saying he *didn't*?"

As he had on the beach, Oscar showed his irritation at being questioned, however he responded, "He did drown. It was obvious, since there was water in his lungs. Gushed everywhere when we got him on the sand."

"Heart attack?" asked Biddy, dropping anchor beside him. "Or maybe just a seizure?"

From his expression it was clear that Oscar did not welcome Biddy's presence. In fact, I'd go so far as to say he disliked her intensely. "I've no idea," he said coldly, drawing back to maximize his personal space.

Biddy grinned at him. "Surprised to see you still here, Oscar. I thought you were leaving this afternoon."

"Something came up." He grabbed his drink from the counter. "Excuse me."

Expressionless, Biddy watched him move away. She turned to me to say, "Keep away from Oscar Fallon. Don't ask me any details — just accept that it's better if you have nothing to do with him."

"I wasn't planning to."

Biddy frowned. "It's not a joke. I know what I'm talking about, okay? He's dangerous."

I put up my hands. "Okay. I don't want anything to do with anyone like that."

Roanna swam into my mind. Well, there was dangerous and there was *dangerous*.

As if I had the power to summon her, Roanna and Pete, chatting like old friends, came walking toward us. "Do you know Roanna Aylmer?" I said to Biddy.

"Never had the pleasure."

"I'm here to relieve you," said Pete. "Roanna tells me it's against federal guidelines to have you chained behind the bar and denied food."

I introduced Biddy to Roanna, and was amused to see them size each other up. A frown creased Roanna's forehead. "I must be losing it," she said. "I prepared tonight's guest list, and I don't recall your name."

"It isn't there," said Biddy. "I talked my way in." She made a wide gesture. "I heard that the Big House was wonderful, and wanted to see it for myself."

"Indeed?"

"You're throwing me out?"

Roanna pursed her lips. "I think not — unless you're here to steal the family silver."

"It's safe. I'm a law-abiding soul. Terminal curiosity is my only sin."

"That killed the cat," said Pete, "but I reckon you'd be harder to dispatch."

Roanna took my arm. "Let's get you something to eat."

I went along willingly. My skin tingled where her fingers had touched me, and I was beginning to have high hopes for this night. So maybe she was just being kind to a starving staff member. I was pretty sure it was more than that. Pete's warning was an encouragement, rather than a deterrent. There was no way I was falling for this woman, so whatever happened was part of my mission. I was here to seduce her, if necessary — I hoped it would be — and find out what I could.

With the thought that I should make a good impression, I managed to limit myself to a moderate pile of fool on my plate, all of it easy to eat. I wasn't about to make a bad impression by ripping a lobster to bits with my bare hands. Grabbing a napkin and a fork, I followed Roanna out of the courtyard and into the gardens.

We were alone. Little paths wound between the displays of ferns, palms and tropical flowers. The full moon swam in a velvet sky, insects made chirping sounds, the fronds rustled. We sat on a stone bench in a sea of warm dark air. "Do eat," said Roanna. "You must be starving."

Wow! It was *so* romantic, if you liked that sort of thing. Normally I was pretty well impervious, but I was suddenly reminded of a scene in *Raw Embers of the Heart,* Denise Hunter's chosen reading. Out of sheer boredom I'd been plowing through it, feeling rather guilty to be almost enjoying the experience, and there was one love scene in the garden of a country estate that had quite raised my temperature after I'd mentally changed the gender of the hero.

My stomach growled. Romance or not, the contents of my plate were irresistible. I did my best to nibble delicately rather than to bolt down the whole lot in one minute flat. My resolve lasted for all of ten seconds, then I decided to hell with it and hoed in. "I have a healthy appetite," I said, swallowing the last mouthful.

"So I see."

Silence. Insects made night noises, the scent of flowers was heavy, the woman beside me glowed in the moonlight. Pete had told me that Roanna didn't live in the Big House, but had a bungalow of her own at the edge of the gardens. If I played my cards right, maybe she'd ask me in for a nightcap. I rehearsed what I might say to subtly encourage an invitation, but I came up blank. This was not like me, and I had to face the possibility that Roanna Aylmer had achieved the impossible and had rendered me speechless.

She said, "I'm going sailing tomorrow. Do you want to come?"

"I've got a shift starting at ten in the morning."

"I've already changed it to the afternoon."

"Just like that?"

"Just like that."

Now this was irritating. "Are you so sure I'd say yes?"

"You haven't said yes yet."

Hoping the moonlight was bright enough for her to clearly see my cheeky grin, I said, "I'm flattered, but why me?"

"I don't feel like being alone."

I didn't respond, having found that technique to have worked before. Roanna said sardonically, "Are you waiting to be assured you'll be paid double time?"

"What the hell," I said, "I'll do it for free."

Roanna's lips curved. "That's a pleasant surprise. You looked very expensive to me."

CHAPTER SEVEN

Sunday morning Jen caught me in the ablutions block when I emerged, yawning, from the shower. "Den! Did you see her?"

"Are you stalking me?"

She stared at me, perplexed. "Half the time I don't know what you're talking about."

I wound my towel around my wet hair and tucked the ends in to form a turban. It was clear Jen was going to bug me until I told her what I knew. "You've got nothing to worry about. Her name's Cynthia

Urquhart. She's in her late thirties and much taller than he is."

Relief washed across Jen's face. "She's old, then? And too tall. Good."

"Not his type at all, unless she's got a lot of money." My dry tone was lost on Jen, who was leaning forward to examine her face closely in the nearest mirror. "I'm thinking of getting tinted contacts," she said. "What do you think?"

"I'd go for purple, if I were you."

I didn't move fast enough. Jen's elbow jabbed me in the ribs. "Oh, *you*!" she said.

It was hard to visualize Jen and Quint Aylmer together, romantically or otherwise, although rumor had it that she was sensational in bed. That could have been very true, for all I knew, and certainly explained Quint Aylmer's interest.

A little girlish heart-to-heart wouldn't hurt, I decided. Steeling myself, I said, "What do you and Quint talk about?"

After checking that no one was nearby, Jen said, "Oh, you know."

"Well, I don't actually. Do you discuss the resort? The weather? Football? Your future together?" I felt a bit guilty about that last one, as I was sure that the likelihood of Jen accomplishing a lasting relationship with Quint Aylmer was close to a snowball's chance in hell.

She was back regarding her reflection. "He talks about family stuff," she said. "Like, what goes on, and how he wants to run the business himself, but his dad and mum won't give him a chance."

"What about Harry?"

"Harry?" Her voice was loaded with scorn. "Like,

he puts Quint down, every chance he gets. Says Roanna's the smart one."

Smart enough to get an advanced degree, I thought. "So Quint and Harry don't get on?"

Jen licked a finger and carefully smoothed one eyebrow. "Sort of. Their mum makes them. That's the problem, you see. Everyone in the family is scared of her. What she says, goes. Quint's afraid she won't approve of me, so we're keeping it really quiet. Secret."

Since I'd bet that every single staff member knew about Jen's affair with the youngest son, I had severe doubts that this would remain hidden from his mother much longer.

Swinging around to face me, Jen said, "Where are you going this morning? I've been told to fill in for your ten o'clock shift."

"Sorry. I had nothing to do with it."

"It's okay." Her glance sharpened. "So what are you doing?"

It wasn't a classified information. Besides, I might get some interesting response. I said, "I'm going sailing with Roanna."

"Are you?" Jen looked thoughtful. "Of course you know she's a lesbian. You'd think the Aylmers would care, wouldn't you, but they don't. She has affairs all the time." She gave me a conspiratorial wink. "Good luck!"

The little vessel flew over the pastel water like a dragonfly, seeming barely to touch the surface. "Hey," I said, "shouldn't we be wearing life jackets?"

"I thought you'd be the kind to live dangerously."

"It's the living part of that I'm interested in."

She brought the yacht about, and the boom nearly scalped me as I ducked. She said, "So am I."

I'd lost the point. "What?"

"Interested in living to the full."

I didn't bite, although she seemed to be waiting for some response. In silence, we headed for one of the tiny islands. It consisted of a knot of greenery, a narrow crescent of beach and a collection of palm trees. "Has this been artificially created?" I asked. "I mean, it's just like an island in a cartoon."

"It's natural," said Roanna, "but there's no water, so it's pretty, but useless."

"Ah," I said, "just what my mother always said about me."

Roanna shot me a sudden, delighted smile. "I really like you, Denise," she said. "You're not quite like anyone else."

"Nor are you, I suspect."

For some reason, that light comment sobered her, and our inconsequential banter came to a stop. Then she was fully occupied with sailing as the yacht heeled over to a stiff breeze from the east. I contemplated her: she was sexy as hell, and had a brooding quality that was probably a pain in real life but added to her allure at the moment. She hadn't kissed me last night in the garden, just said a cool good-night. This omission had annoyed me no end, but I'd decided she had to make the first move. It was always better in these situations to be the pursued, rather than the pursuer. Besides, for someone like Roanna, it was likely the chase was the exciting thing, and she'd tire of me once she caught me.

I leaned back in the little cockpit and enjoyed the day. The water hissed under the keel, the sail thrummed, the ocean glittered. As if on cue, two dolphins broke the surface beside us. Overhead, white seabirds sailed on an updraft.

I glanced at my watch. "I've got to get back."

My contact, Malcolm Endicott, would have arrived on the island by now. He would go to the cocktail lounge, see I wasn't on duty, and fill in time by walking on the beach or visiting one of the little boutiques that sold outrageously priced items to a captive audience or sitting in the trendy coffee shop, irritatingly named Jitterbug Café, where caffeine was similarly expensive. He'd return to the bar for the beginning of the next shift, and I intended to be there to meet him.

"I've got to get back," I said again.

"You don't."

"My shift starts soon." I was emphatic. "Please."

Her mouth settled into a sulky line. I imagined kissing her lips into a smile. Without a word she tacked, then tacked again, beating our way back to the brilliant green of Aylmer Island.

She ran us expertly up to the mooring, dropping the sail at just the right point so that we slowed enough for me to snag the buoy with a boat hook. She signaled imperiously to the guy on the dock, who immediately swung down into a dinghy and started for us. Roanna frowned at me. "I wasn't ready to come back."

"You can go out again by yourself."

"No."

"Do you expect to always get your own way?" I asked.

"Usually. I didn't with you." Her cool expression dissolved into a warm smile. "At least, not this time."

Malcolm was in a group of day-trippers who spilled into the bar, talking in loud voices. It was a comfort to see his familiar face. His sunburned nose was peeling, and he wore a bright Hawaiian shirt, shorts and sandals. This was such a contrast to the sober suit I usually saw him wearing that I had to repress a smile.

"Beer, love," Malcolm said, elbowing another generic day-tripper out of the way so he could settle at the bar.

"Foster's okay?" I said. It was a simple code. If I nominated Foster's beer, it meant that I had something to pass to him.

I gave him his beer and served the others lining up along the bar. When I got back to Malcolm he was wiping his mouth with the back of one reddened hand. "I'll have the same again."

When I came back with his second beer, he said, "Hot enough for you?" That indicated that he had written information to pass to me.

In training we'd been through the next bit a hundred times. Malcolm fished around for his wallet in his back pocket, taking it out with a creased white schedule for the ferry service to the mainland. He extracted a twenty from his wallet and slapped it down for the drinks. "Love, can you point out the time for the next ferry for me?"

"Sure. I'll get your change first."

When Malcolm and I had been practicing, I'd seen

myself on video doing the changeover until it looked completely natural. I got the change, fumbled with the schedule and dropped it, bent down to scoop it up, and went back to the counter. "Here," I said, pointing to the schedule I'd exchanged, "you'll see the next one leaves in twenty minutes."

The report I'd passed to Malcolm gave the details I'd overheard regarding the shipping of illegal immigrants and stated that I'd had some social contact with Roanna. I asked for any additional information on Snead and requested deep background on Biddy, Oscar, and Lainie Snead. As an afterthought I'd added Cynthia Urquhart to the list.

Malcolm stayed in the lounge for a few minutes, getting into a friendly argument about football with a couple of other guys. He didn't look at me again, and I felt oddly abandoned when he walked out the door.

I continued smiling brightly and providing drinks to an apparently endless succession of touristy people. Instead of feeling pleased that the contact had gone off without a hitch, I felt restless and impatient. The ASIO communication seemed to glow in the pocket of my shorts, as though advertising its illicit presence. I wouldn't have the opportunity to look at it until later, and anyway, I was fairly sure it would contain a reminder that one of my major tasks was to find out more about the upcoming international conference the resort was hosting.

The conference was scheduled to start in two days, and I was no closer to getting information on the program or the guests. I knew that most attendees were coming from Asian countries, and that the conference was billed as an exploration of the future applications of the Internet to international trade, but that was all. I'd been cultivating Vera because of her position of convention facilitator, but all I'd got so far was a litany of her problems and a life history that was, if possible, even more boring than her complaints about the people she worked with in the convention center. Unfortunately Vera had total recall, and she was able to resurrect at a moment's notice every slight and upset she'd suffered, even from years before.

Girding myself to do my duty, I called her on the internal phone when my shift ended. I suggested that we meet at the hideously expensive coffee shop in the middle of the row of trendy boutiques, thinking that if I had to put up with Vera, at least I could treat myself to some elaborate caffeine kick.

"Coffee?" she whined. "I don't think so. I've got so much work to do, it just isn't fair."

"I'll come over."

Although I'd studied the layout of the resort, I'd never been inside the convention center. All wood and glass, it was built on an octagonal design, with conference rooms radiating from a central core that held the hospitality areas. One segment of the wheel was reserved for administration, and I had to sign in before I could enter that section.

"Who are you here to see?" asked the guard, checking my signature and then my name tag. "Denise," he added. His tag indicated that he was Doug. I'd never seen him before, so I guessed he was part of the Big House security.

"Well, Doug," I said, "I'm here to see Vera Otterlage."

"And your business with her?"

"I'm a friend."

A look of mild astonishment crossed Doug's face, which told me he knew Vera well enough to wonder why anyone would chose to be friends with her. "That way," he said, pointing. "Third office on the left."

I found Vera in a small cubicle, peering with a vexed expression into a monitor. "I don't know why they can't have normal spelling," she said. "I mean, you can't even pronounce half of their names."

Looking over her shoulder I saw information set out in columns. "This for the conference the day after tomorrow?"

She nodded absently. "I've got to do the name tags for the attendees," she said, "and I daren't make a mistake with the spelling, you know. People are just so particular about that." Her tone made it clear she considered this demand for accuracy unreasonable.

Pulling up a spare chair, I said, "Can I help?"

Vera's protruding blue eyes mirrored astonished gratitude. I had to believe she rarely, if ever, had anyone offer to assist her. She was so irritating, I doubt I would have, under normal circumstances. "Denise, that would be rilly nice of you."

At least she didn't call me Den. I sat down with a printout and started going through the list with her, checking spelling against application documents. I was alert for anyone I might recognize. It was clear that there was a wide selection of Asian business people, but one name leapt out at me: Farid Sabir. He was an immensely influential Indonesian entrepreneur who had international business interests. Lately there'd been rumors that he was testing the water for a political career, and this had caused quite a lot of turmoil in backrooms in several Asian countries.

I swore to myself, wishing that I'd known this in

time to give the information to Malcolm. Almost certainly the authorities had been alerted that Sabir was about to enter the country, but I was uneasy about his presence on Aylmer Island. He'd survived one assassination attempt in London earlier in the year, and Britain had got plenty of flack about that, so there no way the Australian government wanted to cope with even a minor incident here.

My next contact was with an agent called Alice Beher, but she wasn't due until Wednesday, three days away, so unless I had an urgent enough reason to risk a phone call, it would have to wait until then.

"What an interesting job you have," I said to Vera as I corrected yet another of her spelling errors.

She seemed surprised. "You think so?"

"Well, you meet all these important people."

"Usually I don't *meet* them. I mean, I do practically everything for them, but I never get thanked."

I could almost see the bitter resentment that swirled around her. I imagined it would be a sort of pea green, perhaps with red streaks.

Vera was building up steam. "Like, I make sure the accommodations are ready, any special diets are in place, the equipment for the sessions is all there. And if anything goes wrong... Well! Just guess who they blame!"

She flicked the edge of a folder with one finger, the nail of which, I noticed, was bitten to the quick. "And there's all those extras, for instance, the cruise out to see the reef and snorkel round the coral, and all that stuff. I have to make sure that Tim puts the diving equipment on the cat, and then there's the refreshments and the drinks..." She trailed off, apparently overcome with the responsibility of it all.

The cat referred to the catamaran ferry that Aylmer Resort owned. George Aylmer had named it *Moreen* in honor of his wife, and I'd come across from the mainland on it. My first sight of the cat had reminded me of an elaborate toy, rather than the deep sea vessel that it was. Dazzling white with blue trim, it had rocked gently at the wharf, its outsize pontoons looking awkward, like feet that were too large. This impression of clumsiness disappeared as soon as the craft was underway and had gained enough speed to rise up on its floats: Then it attained an awesome speed, skimming on white foam over the crests of the waves. Seb had told me that a larger version held a trans-Atlantic record, and I had no trouble believing him.

It took us the best part of an hour to correct the list, print out the tags and slide each name into a burnished metal holder. Vera wasn't very adept at fine motor tasks, so I did most of them.

"They're not getting hibiscus tags," I said, tapping my own monstrosity on my left breast. I'd always liked hibiscus, but Aylmer Island was spoiling my former enthusiasm for the flower.

"I *know*," said Vera. "It's a shame, isn't it?"

I didn't roll my eyes this time, but being with Vera did, I found, tend to give my eyeball muscles a good workout. Determined to make my suffering with Vera worthwhile, I decided to ask her about Eddie Trebonus, mainly because he was a guest at the Big House, but also because Roanna obviously disliked him, and that was reason enough for me to be interested.

"Do you know Eddie Trebonus?"

"Eddie? Oh yes."

"I've seen him in the bar a lot," I volunteered. "He's always asking for these weird cocktails."

"Eddie's a bit weird himself," said Vera emphatically. "Like, he's always coming 'round here and getting in my way, and making jokes I don't get. But I can't tell him to get lost, you see, because he works for Moreen Aylmer."

"Doing what?"

"Well, I don't know. I know she sends him off to different places because I often I have to do the travel arrangements, which isn't fair, because it rilly isn't part of my duties, you see."

I had to get her back on track before she wallowed in the injustice of it all. I said bracingly, "Obviously you're asked to do the arrangements because you're so competent."

Vera blinked. "I suppose . . ."

"So where does Eddie go?"

"All over. I guess it's something to do with drumming up clients for conferences, because he always comes back and gives a report to Harry and his mother. He usually goes overseas, but this time I booked his flight to Darwin."

A couple of further casual questions showed that Vera didn't know anything more about Eddie, so I filed his name away to add to my list of background requests on the communication I would pass Alice on Wednesday.

"You know Jen?" said Vera.

I felt like snapping "Never heard of her," but instead I gave Vera a heartening smile.

"Well . . ." Vera stared at me, clearly expecting encouragement.

"What about Jen?" I asked, obediently.

"She's going to be upset." Vera was pleased. "Quint Aylmer's practically engaged to someone else." Before I could ask who, Vera went on, "It's a guest."

"Cindy Urquhart?"

Vera was crushed. "You knew!"

"I have my sources."

Looking at me with new respect, Vera said, "So what do you think?"

"About Quint Aylmer? Gosh, I don't know. Have you seen this Cynthia Urquhart?" When Vera shook her head, I said, "She's very tall, and older than him, I think."

"No! Taller than him?"

"Yes, I'm afraid so."

"Gee," said Vera, chagrined. "Kay must have got it wrong, then."

Feeling that I had to stand up for tall sisters, I said, "Why couldn't Quint be having a relationship with someone taller than he is?"

"You know men. They don't like to feel smaller." Vera brightened to add, "But you're right, it could still be true. He does play the field, unlike his brother."

After complaining, there was nothing Vera liked more than a bit of gossip. "You think Harry's more serious?" I said.

"Oh yes. *Much.* He's sort of stern, but he's rilly very nice, you know." She preened herself. "Actually, he's involved in most of the conferences, so we get to work together quite a lot."

"I suppose eventually Harry will take over the running of the resort."

Vera's glanced around, checking if anyone could overhear. "Not if his mother has anything to do with it," she whispered. "Moreen thinks Quint should be the one, even if he is the youngest. Not that her husband agrees. I've heard there's been words exchanged, you know what I mean."

"What about Roanna? Has she been considered?"

Vera's puzzled expression was expected. "Roanna? Why would she even think of running the place?"

As I helped her slot the name tags in alphabetical order, I said casually, "Who are the speakers at this conference? Well-known people? Celebrities?"

Vera scrunched up her face. "I'm not involved in that side of it, fortunately. I do know Roanna's doing a session."

I looked bored. "Yeah?"

"Something about the Internet." She put the tray of tags into the top drawer of a filing cabinet and slammed it shut. "There! We're all finished, and thanks for the help. Now we can go to the Jitterbug for that coffee you promised me."

"Great." I gritted my teeth. I was almost to the point of Vera overload, but I had to persevere, as I had no way of knowing what gems of information she might still have.

She gave me one after we'd both signed out at the security desk. "You know," she said, as we strolled toward the coffee shop, "When I started here I had to sign a strict confidentiality agreement."

"Really?"

Vera, buoyed by my obvious admiration, gave a self-satisfied giggle. "Like, I hear lots of things, but I have to keep them to myself."

"Such as?" I was all encouragement.

She frowned at me. "Tsk! You know I can't tell you."

"Right." In that one word I managed to inject a

potent note of doubt in her veracity, to which Vera immediately responded.

"Oh, all right," she said, "I will tell you one thing, but you've got to promise not to repeat it." She looked around, as though we were under surveillance. I looked around too, thinking maybe we were.

Dropping her voice to a whisper, Vera went on, "They didn't know I could hear, but this afternoon Harry was talking to his mother in the next office, and he was telling her how he'd checked out a guest, and she'd turned out to be a private investigator!"

"No!"

"Yes!" Vera took my arm. "She's here in secret, on a case."

Vera looked mysterious: I knew my expression nicely mingled awe and curiosity. "Go on," I said.

"You know that man who got killed with the shotgun? Well, his family hired this detective, because they don't think it was an accident."

"That's awful," I said. "I mean, what if the guy's family is right, and it wasn't an accident? I suppose the Aylmers are really worried."

"Worried? I don't think so! Harry and his mother were laughing about the whole thing." Vera halted to beam at me. "I bet you can't guess who the detective is."

"Biddy Gallagher," I said.

Vera gave a small scream. "You *knew*! How do you *do* that, Den?"

"A wild guess," I murmured, trying to play down what I'd just done, which was, frankly, to be very stupid. I didn't want Vera burbling away to others about how I was sharp enough, or interested enough, to peg Biddy as the PI, although it hadn't been hard to make an educated guess, since Vera had mentioned the person was a female. Biddy then became the obvious choice, being a former cop who was asking questions about the shooting death.

I could hear my trainer's voice as if he were standing beside me. "Dumb, dumb, dumb," he was saying. "You just had to be a smartarse, didn't you, Denise?"

I read the missive Malcolm had passed to me sitting on the green bench in my little hideaway in the gardens. Deciphering the cryptic notes, I found that Lloyd Snead's lungs had been full of seawater. Why this had happened wasn't clear, as he hadn't suffered any serious injury, heart attack or stroke. There were superficial bruises on both shoulders, possibly caused by the harness of his air tanks. The investigating officers had not been able to locate these tanks to check if they had been faulty. The media had been advised it was an accidental death, but I was to assume that the circumstances were suspicious.

In the coffee shop with Vera, I'd had a quick glance at a Sunday newspaper brought over from the mainland. Snead's death was summed up in one sentence in the breaking news digest: *Lloyd Snead, international banker, died Friday in a drowning accident at Aylmer Island luxury resort.*

I expected that there would be much more comment in the Monday papers, particularly in the financial sections, as Snead had been well-known for wheeling and dealing on the international stage. From my earlier ASIO briefings I knew of one activity Snead had managed to keep under wraps — his career in money laundering. This was about to change. Snead had had extensive contacts with Russian banks, and his name had come up in ongoing investigations carried out by several countries concerning the transfer of huge sums of money from Russia to banking institutions all over the world. The scandal was that the money was international aid, intended to help the ailing Russian economy.

The other information raised my eyebrows. The CIA had very recently put an operative in place on Aylmer Island. There was no name, or even an indication of gender. I understood the game: All security organizations kept as much from other agencies as possible, even within their own countries. More, they kept as much secret as they could from the governments who set them up.

I checked the nearby path to make sure no one was anywhere near me before I burned the communication. Then I carefully mashed the ashes into the dirt under a shrub, dusted my hands, and set off for a scintillating evening in the rec room.

"There's an envelope for you," Kay said the moment she saw me. She was obviously dressed to go out: she wore much makeup, and her dress was in shades of cream and brown to complement her hair. "Like it?" she asked, twirling around.

After the grueling time I'd had with Vera, I didn't feel gracious enough to fake interest. "Lovely," I said shortly.

Enthusiasm undaunted, Kay said, "Some of us are popping over to the mainland for a bit of a party.

You've got time to change if you like to join us. Actually, Bruce was looking for you earlier, to ask you to come, but he couldn't find you."

I thought *Thank you, Vera* as I said, "Bruce didn't mean as his date, did he?"

"I'd say so." Kay smirked at my horror. "Jeez, Den, don't you like him?"

"He's all yours, Kay. He's too much man for me."

She went off laughing, turning at the rec room door to call out, "Don't forget your message."

The envelope had my name in unfamiliar writing, strong and angular. Retreating to the bland surroundings of my bedroom, I slit open the envelope. The single page was from Roanna, and was very brief: *Denise, I'm asking you to a private picnic tomorrow. I'll provide everything. Pick you up at eleven. Roanna.*

CHAPTER EIGHT

The next morning Roanna turned up twenty minutes early, announcing her presence with a sharp rap on my door. She was dressed as I was, in shorts and a T-shirt. Her top was plain, crisp white, mine was pale green with the words GRAVITY! NOT JUST A GOOD IDEA, BUT THE LAW.

Ridiculously, I was embarrassed to have her see the banal little room I slept in, so I came out into the corridor, hastily closing the door behind me. "Okay, I'm yours."

She grinned but didn't comment. She handed me

an insulated backpack, the twin of the one she wore, and we set off into the clear morning air. It was warm rather than hot, and the sunlight didn't have its usual metallic force.

We strolled down the path from the staff quarters, passing Seb going the other way. "Hi," he said, eyeing Roanna and then me. A smile turned the corners of his mouth. "Have a nice day."

I gave him a stern look. "We'll try."

His knowing smile turned into a laugh. "I bet you will."

As we continued, Roanna said, as though she'd never seen Seb before, "A friend of yours?"

I looked at her with surprise. "Don't you know Seb? He's worked on the island for over two years."

"I know him by sight, that's all. I don't have that much to do with the day-to-day running of the resort."

We walked along in silence for a moment, then I said, "What do you do?"

Her mouth tightened. "You mean, am I gainfully employed, or just sponging off my family?"

Hell! I didn't want to alienate Roanna — I was supposed to be gaining her trust. I spread my hands in a don't-misunderstand-me gesture. "I was interested, that's all."

Mollified, she said, "Sorry, I took your question the wrong way. I look after the computer side of things for the resort. I set up the accounting system, I keep the Web page up-to-date, and on the Internet I handle bookings, queries, advertising, all that sort of thing."

"Gosh," I said. "Over my head, I'm afraid."

As we reached the shoreline edge of the Aylmer compound, Tony, the nasty drunk from the bar whom Roanna had told to get lost at the party last night, was walking from the beach, scuba tanks in one hand. Seeing Roanna, he made a wide detour so that he wouldn't pass close to us.

"That guy," I said, "Tony, isn't it? I don't like him."

Roanna sent a scornful look in his direction. "I share your opinion. But the trouble is, he's a friend of Harry and Quint's, so I have to put up with him." She gave me a wry smile. "Frankly, I don't much like most of my brothers' friends."

There was an opening, but I didn't want to seem to be pushing her for information. "Yeah, I know what you mean," I said, commiserating. "My brother had any number of friends I couldn't stand."

We traded thoughts about brothers, and families in general, and I started to fill in the details of the Aylmer relationships. As I'd already been told, although George Aylmer was the titular head, his wife, Moreen, was most emphatically in charge, with nothing happening that she didn't know about. She ran the company with the help of her two sons: Harry doing most of the work, Quint the golden boy in his mother's eyes. Roanna seemed to be on the periphery of the action, being occupied with the computer side of things but not involved in any decision making.

Hope began to bloom in me that Roanna might not know about the criminal activities. I had to acknowledge that this optimism was hardly justified. She was clearly intelligent, and it was difficult to believe that she had remained ignorant of everything that was going on around her.

We were walking along a narrow path a few meters in from the shoreline. At the beginning it was posted as being a private way. We came to a junction, where another path ran away from the water. "That leads to my little house," said Roanna.

I was curious. "Can I have a look?"

"Sure, but you won't see much."

I'd been surreptitiously examining the boundaries of the Aylmer compound on my daily walks. A light mesh fence, two meters high, ran along the borders I'd explored, and I was positive that an alarm would go off if anyone attempted to get in. I hadn't looked at this lower boundary, and I wanted to check if it was the same.

It was only a few steps to a tall security gate. I peered through its mesh and caught the merest glimpse of a building nestling in the greenery.

"Just a few steps to the ocean," I said. "Now that's luxury."

We strolled on, chatting about nothing in particular — music, movies we'd seen, funny things that had happened to us in the past. I found myself elated to be in her company, enjoying the experience as if I had no hidden agenda and Roanna didn't belong to a family almost certainly responsible for crimes as heinous as murder and sedition.

After half an hour or so we came to a pristine little beach, deserted except for a couple of raffish seagulls who were having a vulgar screaming match over a prized morsel. Roanna dropped her pack on the sand and made a wide gesture. "How about here?"

"Good enough."

It was better than good. Aquamarine water edged the white sand; the sky arched pale blue and brazen above us; a tiny tree snake, like a brilliant green ribbon, curled around the branch of a tree. A couple of incandescent blue-and-black butterflies played tag.

One could, I thought, tire of such perfection eventually, or at least take it for granted, but for me the scenery on this island had a charmed, not-quite-real atmosphere about it, as though magic was in the air and spells and enchantments were commonplace. I had to admit that I was a smidgen enchanted by Roanna.

We sat down in the shade of a clump of palms. She said, "It's a Spartan picnic, but nourishing, I assure you."

It wasn't in the least Spartan, of course. There were delightful little individual packages, and opening each one was like unwrapping a gift. Appetizers of smoked salmon and capers, and pâté and crackers, were followed by chicken and ham and rare roast beef, each one accompanied by side dishes to enhance its flavor.

The insulated pack had kept the wine cold, and it filled my mouth with astringent coolness. "A toast," I said, clinking my plastic glass against hers. "Let's drink to . . ." I paused, then went on, "To good fortune."

In a weak moment, I'd almost said, *Let's drink to us.*

We finished the wine, neatly packed everything away, and then sat side by side contemplating the water. "Nice day," I said, taking off my sunglasses and turning my head to look at her lips. Looking at someone's mouth is supposed to make the person want to kiss you. It had worked for me before, but I wasn't sure if Roanna was susceptible.

She was.

We leaned toward each other, without haste. Our lips touched once, tentatively, then we were kissing desperately, as though our hunger could never be satisfied. We slid down, until we were lying on the sand. She tasted wonderful, wonderful. I tingled, flamed, grew tight.

"Crikey, you can kiss," I said, breaking away for air.

She was as breathless as I was. With a mischievous grin, she said, "I've been practicing, just for you."

I pulled her to me, turning until she was on top of me. "Now I've got you where I want you," she said as she lowered her mouth to mine. God! If this was kissing, what would lovemaking be like? I couldn't keep still, or quiet. I arched under her, groaned, put my hands around the back of her neck and devoured her mouth.

This was way out of control. The last rational part of me was pointing out that we were on a beach, where anyone might come by, but my body didn't care about that at all. "I want more," I said against her lips.

Roanna was more circumspect than me, or perhaps she had better hearing. She lifted her head. "Someone's coming."

"What?"

Then I could hear them too. A group, it sounded like, talking and laughing as they came closer to us. By the time they came out onto the beach we were sitting side by side again, chastely admiring the scenery. We were flushed and hot, but hey, this was the tropics.

"Hi," said one young girl, a greeting that was echoed by her three companions, another girl and two young gangly boys, a greeting of sweet awkwardness that youth grow out of far too quickly.

We hied back.

It was clear that they were going to settle on our beach. They chose a spot just along from us and dumped their things. I looked at the sand we had churned with out activities and said to Roanna, "Perhaps we should go back."

"Perhaps we should."

I couldn't take my eyes off her face, her neck, her bare legs. "I'm sorry we had to stop," I said in a low voice, a precaution that was hardly necessary, since the kids were chattering together like galahs.

"Me too." When she smiled, a dimple appeared in one cheek. I wanted to lean over and kiss it.

Get a grip, Denise!

Excellent. I was in control again, and could probably walk without my knees wobbling. "Okay," I said, leaping up with extraordinary energy, "we've done the beach bit, so what's next?"

Roanna said, "My bed."

A shaft of fire transfixed me. "It's awfully sudden," I said. "I'll have to give it some thought." *Like one millisecond.*

She collected the packs and handed one to me. "Tomorrow night?"

I wanted to say, "Why not *now*, right now!" but that would seem overeager, and I reminded myself I was supposed to be playing this cool. I remarked, "Tomorrow? I'll have to check my appointment diary."

She chuckled. "You do that."

Why tomorrow night? Why not tonight? I hadn't asked while I'd had an Irish coffee with Roanna at the

Jitterbug Café, but impatience throbbed in my over-zealous body, to the point where I'd had to speak severely to myself to stop an impetuous question, or, much worse, a plea.

We said good-bye, and I set off briskly, having to hurry back to my room to change clothes, as I could hardly turn up for my afternoon shift behind the bar with a message T-shirt and without my name tag.

I was passing the clinic, a neat wooden building half hidden by flowering bushes and located near the northern wing of the hotel, when I heard raised voices. "I want that information, and I want it now," boomed Biddy Gallagher.

Whoever she was speaking to murmured something, to which Biddy responded, "Bullshit!"

Curious, I slowed, then made an abrupt turn and headed for the back of the building, where another huge clump of bushes could provide adequate cover. It was fortunate that it was a mild day, because instead of air conditioning, the hinged windows were all open, which explained why I had heard Biddy so clearly.

She was still going strong. "I'll have your license yanked. And that's the best that'll happen to you."

Ivy Bestlove said with her usual calm tone, "As I've said, I can't release confidential medical information to you, Ms. Gallagher. If you wish to take the matter further, I suggest you contact the proper authorities. In the meantime, I would appreciate it if you left."

There was silence, and then the slam of a door. I peered around the side of the building to see Biddy stalking off, her arms swinging. I went around to the front and said through the open window, "Heavens, Ivy, what was that all about? I was passing, and I couldn't help hearing Biddy Gallagher yelling at the top of her voice."

Ivy looked fed up. "You know the woman?"

"I sure do. She's in the bar a lot of the time." I put a strong note of disapproval into my voice.

Ivy nodded. "Maybe that's it. She's had too much to drink."

A quick check of my watch showed I only had five minutes to spare. I opened the door and stepped into the front room of the clinic. "Are you okay?"

Ivy seemed surprised I would even ask. "Of course."

"So what has upset Biddy?"

Obviously wearied by Biddy's frontal attack, Ivy said, "The blasted woman was trying to bully me about the shotgun death you've no doubt heard all about."

"It was an accident, wasn't it? Someone tripped or fell or something, and the gun went off."

"That's right. It was a woman who pulled the trigger. She was hysterical, so they brought her to me to calm her down. Her name was Fountain, Aileen Fountain."

Acting puzzled, I said, "But why would Biddy Gallagher be interested in that?"

"Some investigation, she claimed. Tried to tell me she was a cop, but when I asked for her identification, she changed her story and admitted she was some sort of private investigator." Ivy gave me a grim smile. "So I told her to get lost."

"But what was she asking you about?"

"Whether Aileen Fountain was showing classic signs of shock — shaking, confusion, hysteria. What you'd expect if you'd just killed someone in an accident. I told Ms. Gallagher it was none of her business."

It wasn't mine either, but I said, "And *was* the Fountain woman in shock?"

Ivy looked at me quizzically. "She put on a good performance, but if you'd asked when I examined her, I'd have had to say to you, No, she isn't in shock at all."

I made it to the Tropical Heat with a minute to spare. Pete was usually rostered on with me, but to my dismay I found that I was going to be sharing the space behind the bar with Bruce. "Hi, Den," Bruce said with what he no doubt considered a winning smile. "Pete wanted the afternoon off, and I agreed to swap with him."

Making a mental note to punch Pete in the mouth when next I saw him, I said without enthusiasm, "Great." This was going to be a long shift. Bruce kept staring at me with his unnerving black eyes, and he appeared to be toning down his sneer. This was not good.

I'd never worked with Bruce before, thank God, so I was expecting the worst. I thought, for example, that he would be a dead loss as a bartender because I was sure that when he wasn't propping his compact, solid body against the counter to chat up the nearest female, he'd be helping himself to the alcohol. As the cocktail lounge filled up, I was pleasantly astonished to find neither was true: Bruce worked quite efficiently, only gulped down one drink on the sly that I saw, and didn't try charming any of our many customers. This last item may have been because he was trying to charm *me*.

"Den," he said when we ran into each other near the register, "you've got a boyfriend, have you?"

"Girlfriend." When he frowned, I snapped, "You should be asking if I have a *girlfriend*. I don't go with men."

I congratulated myself that I'd turned Bruce off, but the next time we passed, he said, "A girlfriend's okay. I don't mind a threesome." He winked. "Know what I mean?"

"No way," I said, but Bruce was already down to the other end of the bar.

An hour later I cornered him by the glass-washer. "What part of the word *lesbian* don't you understand? That's what I am. Okay?"

Bruce wasn't fazed. "Jen told me you were really bi," he said. "Swinging both ways — it's a good way to be."

"Oh *please!*" Bruce looked at me expectantly. "Look," I said, "you'll be the first to know, but I've got a girlfriend *and* a boyfriend, so you see, regretfully, I have to turn you down." Of course, I had neither, but desperate situations require desperate measures.

His eyes narrowed to dark slits, Bruce said, "Who's the guy?"

"I can't say. It's a secret."

"Do I know him?"

Maybe this hadn't been that good an idea. "I told you, I can't say."

Bruce grunted and moved to serve someone who was tapping impatiently on the bar. My night was complete: It was Eddie Trebonus.

"Den!" he said, angling his head so he could look around Bruce. "I'm back. Did you miss me?"

Bruce gave me a meaningful look that said, *So this is the boyfriend.*

"Bruce is a whiz with cocktails," I said, escaping to the back behind the shelves where I could indulge in a hysterical laugh.

CHAPTER NINE

Tonight's the night, I thought the moment I opened my eyes on Tuesday morning. It was a pity I hadn't come up with a phrase more literary, more romantic, but it was the best I could do. I had a morning shift to work, an afternoon to fill, and then Roanna and the evening waited.

I fought the temptation to curl up and fantasize about Roanna. Why not hurry through the day and taste the real thing? I sat up, resolute, to make a mental list of people to avoid at all costs, and people to seek out. Bruce and Eddie were definitely in the to-be-avoided column; Biddy, Vera and Lainie Snead, if I could find her, belonged in the second group.

Showered, dressed and mildly exercised — I tried to use the staff gym room at least twice a week — I went in search of Vera and found her eating breakfast in the rec room, her jaws moving rhythmically as she watched the television screen.

"Good morning, Vera."

My good cheer was wasted. Vera acknowledged me with a wave of a hand but continued to watch the program. I stood looming over her until she reluctantly tore her gaze away. "Hi, Den. This is my favorite show."

"I thought you'd be hard at work in the convention center already," I said heartily, "what with all the people coming in today for the conference."

Her attention had returned to the screen, where a blonde with impossibly large breasts and an impossibly small waist was telling a guy almost as pretty as herself that she loved him more than he could ever know.

"I'm working late tonight, so I don't go in until noon," Vera said.

The show went to a commercial break that featured dancing shampoo bottles and more anatomically incorrect females with lustrous, long hair.

I said, "So all the attendees are coming? There's no probs?"

"They're all coming." Her face crumpled a little. "I mean, it's only thirty people, but you've no idea how much work it is for me. Practically every person has different diet requirements, and then, of course, no one told me until yesterday that one of them is bringing three bodyguards, so I have to find extra accommodation, and that was a pain."

"Wow," I said. "Three bodyguards. Is it someone I'd know?"

"I doubt it. Mr. Sabir. He was here last year and he didn't bring any bodyguards, so I don't see why he needs them now."

Her gaze was wrenched back to the screen by a burst of violin music. The same pneumatic blonde and handsome guy were still looking into each other's eyes. "It's really sad," said Vera. "She doesn't know that she's got a brain tumor or that he's her brother. Separated at birth, they were."

I shook my head, but Vera didn't notice, so I went in search of breakfast.

In the first hours of the morning shift the Tropical Heat had few customers, which was fortunate since I was the only one on duty. Biddy Gallagher came in as soon as I opened the doors, the morning paper under her arm. "They're making a big deal over the guy who drowned on Friday," she said to me, indicating the lead story on the front page. DEAD BANKER SCANDAL was the main headline, followed by the subheading, LINK TO RUSSIAN BANKS?

To make up for my past insensitivity about Lainie Snead, at least as far as Biddy was concerned, I said, "It was bad enough before for his wife, but this must be dreadful."

Biddy nodded curtly, sat down at her usual table, and said, "I'll have my usual heart-starter."

I would never understand how someone could drink whiskey in the first place, and certainly not straight after breakfast. Of course, in Biddy's case, maybe it *was* her breakfast.

I set the Haig in front of her, and lingered for a chat. Biddy glared at me. "Yes?"

"I was wondering if you've seen Lainie Snead around."

"And why would you be interested if I had?"

"I spoke to her at the party on Saturday night. She looked scared, and I wondered why."

"She's not in the hotel," said Biddy. "They're keeping her in seclusion up at the Big House."

"Keeping her?"

Biddy gave a short laugh. "I'm not suggesting Lainie is a prisoner. It's probably the best place for her, since she undoubtedly knows more about her husband's affairs than would be healthy."

She opened her paper, clearly signaling the end of our conversation. I said, "Ivy Bestlove says you're a private investigator."

An expression of mingled chagrin and embarrassment crossed Biddy's face. "Yes, I made a bit of a bloody fool of myself there."

"I wondered why you were asking me all those questions about the skeet-shooting accident," I said.

Folding the paper, she put it beside her drink, then leaned back in her chair to regard me critically. "You were asking a lot of questions yourself, Denise."

"I'm just interested in things, I suppose."

My airy tone obviously didn't impress Biddy. "I'm not sure what you're playing at," she said, "but don't ever think I'm a fool."

"I don't." Now was the time to give her something

in the hope that she would trade something in return. "I was walking past the clinic and overheard your argument with Ivy Bestlove," I said. "That's how I know about it. After you left, I talked to her, and she gave me the information you were after."

Biddy tapped a tattoo on the side of her glass. "And what information would that be?"

"About Aileen Fountain. I can give you the answer — Ivy is quite sure that the woman wasn't genuinely in shock, although she tried to act that way."

"So it was a hit." Biddy nodded slowly. "I'm not surprised. Bellamy knew too much." She gave me a dry smile. "Now I suppose I owe you one."

It was pleasing to know she understood the unwritten rules. "On Saturday night you warned me about Oscar Fallon. I want to know why."

She tilted her head, considering. "Okay," she said, "this may or may not be of interest to you, but Fallon is CIA." She waited for my reaction. When there wasn't one, she went on, "I ran into him on a case years ago, when I was in the Federal Police. To say we didn't hit it off is an understatement." Her mouth stretched in a wolfish smile. "Perhaps you can imagine his reaction when we ran into each other here on the island. He took me aside and threatened me with God-knows-what if I blew his cover."

"You're blowing his cover now."

"And it feels good," said Biddy.

My day didn't pass quickly. I finished my shift, had lunch, wandered around the shops, had a coffee at Jitterbug, told Pete I'd break his kneecaps if he left me with Bruce again, and in late afternoon unobtrusively watched as the catamaran docked with the incoming conference attendees on board.

Farid Sabir wasn't hard to identify: He was the short man with the three bulky guys close around him, their stance indicating they were ready to leap into action, as their eyes constantly scanned for signs of trouble. This behavior looked rather ridiculous on a little white-painted wharf with calm water lapping the beach and palm trees sighing gently in a soft breeze. Then I remembered another perfect day, with Lloyd Snead lying on the sand, and it didn't seem so ludicrous at all.

At last, shaved, showered and with the cleanest of clean teeth, I headed for the Aylmer compound. It was near sunset when Roanna met me at the main security gate, which was guarded by two high-mounted cameras I hadn't noticed on the night of the party. They unnerved me by swiveling to follow my progress as I came up the drive. I looked up at them, imagining my image appearing on some security screen somewhere in the Big House. I hoped whoever was looking at it appreciated my freshly-pressed white jeans and cobalt blue top.

"Surely an overreaction," I said to Roanna, pointing at the cameras. "After all, you are on your own island."

"Paranoia runs in the family," she said. "That's the only explanation I can give."

I followed her to the bungalow. Surrounded by wild gardens that were no doubt carefully planted, but seemed like natural growth, the building was constructed of gray-stained wood and had a low thatched roof. Beside it, looking out of place, was a satellite dish, its face turned expectantly to the sky. "You watch a lot of television?" I said.

"Actually, I don't. That's my own personal satellite link for my computer. There's a bigger dish on the roof of the convention center, but I wanted my own private one."

"So other people's grubby little messages didn't get caught up with yours?"

She grinned at me. "Something like that."

The little house had a veranda, just as I'd visualized it, but I hadn't put in the hot tub that entirely took up one end of it. "Perhaps we'll try it later," said Roanna, following my glance.

She took me inside through double glass doors. The floor was polished wood with bright, woven rugs, the furniture simple and sleek. The living room had huge windows showing a sweep of beach and the restless surface of the sea.

The kitchen was small but state of the art. The bathroom tiled in dark blue, had a picture window framing a view of the baby cliff that defined the end of the beach. "No one can look in," she said. "It's one-way glass."

I stood at the bedroom door, but didn't go in. I had a strange feeling that I was intruding on the real Roanna, the person under the façade. The room was, like the rest of the house, beautiful in its simplicity. The bed was positioned so that Roanna could glimpse the sea through a curtain of lush vegetation. One wall was shelves, packed with books, hardcover and paperback.

I went back into the living room. "This is lovely," I said. "If this were mine, I'd never want to leave."

A beautifully wrought Thai partition separated a

little nook that held a computer and monitor. "Where I do most of my work," said Roanna. "If you don't mind, I have an urgent e-mail to send, and then I can forget work altogether."

Any work e-mail was of interest to me, so I casually leaned one hand on the back of her chair and watched her log on. I saw that her e-mail identifying name was *Aylmer5*. She looked up at me with a grin. "One to four went to more senior members of the family on the island," she said. "I'm the runt of the litter."

I smiled, watching closely as she keyed in her password. Most people selected passwords that were easy to remember, including their own names or birth dates. Roanna was no exception: her fingers spelled out *Roanna*.

"A speaker has dropped out of a convention we're hosting next month," she said as she typed the e-mail message, "and we're desperately trying to find a fill-in. This guy I'm contacting is dull as hell, but he knows his stuff."

"What *is* his stuff?"

She frowned at the screen. Correcting a mistake she'd made, she said, "Electronic surveillance."

Taking a chance that she wouldn't think it strange that I would be interested in the subject, I said, "I got the impression the resort was pretty well up-to-date in the surveillance area."

"It is. That's Harry's baby. He's totally paranoid about the subject."

It was too dangerous to ask why, because then she might begin to wonder why I was asking questions on the topic, but Roanna obligingly continued, "I told

Harry I wouldn't put it past him to have this place bugged."

Jeez! The thought had never occurred to me. I did a quick review of what I'd said. Nothing, surely, incriminating.

"In fact," said Roanna, with a grim smile, "I trusted my dear brother so little, that even though he swore he'd never try surveillance on me, I had an expert come over from the mainland and sweep the place for bugs."

She laughed at my expression. "Nothing," she said. "For once Harry told the truth."

This was an interesting conflict between brother and sister, and I would have pursued it, but Roanna concentrated on writing her e-mail. She checked the text, then put the cursor on *Send* and dispatched it to the sea of electronic messages invisibly zipping around the globe.

"Are you hungry?" Roanna asked.

Hungry for you, I thought. "A bit," I said.

"Of course." She grinned. "I'd forgotten that healthy appetite of yours."

We sat out on the veranda in the darkening air. The night fell with tropical suddenness, the colors of the day fading quickly into blue-gray and black. A silver path led across the sea to the full moon rising out of the water. Fruit bats were silhouetted as they swooped and dived. I sipped the French champagne she'd offered me, although I needed nothing alcoholic to intoxicate me when I had Roanna to do that, gleaming in the dying light, her face for the first time relaxed rather than watchful.

She saluted me with her glass. "To the evening."

"Not the entire night?"

She chuckled, then raised her glass again. "To the entire night."

Now that I was there with her, I was in no hurry. We talked a little, but most of the time we were silent, part of the living darkness. We went inside to eat, sitting opposite each other at the kitchen bench. Roanna had prepared a chopped salad to go with roast chicken. My appetite, usually robust, had all but disappeared.

"Don't you like it?" asked Roanna, indicating my hardly touched plate.

"For once, I'm not hungry." *But famished for you.*

She offered me a liqueur, but I declined. "I don't drink much."

"A good quality in a bartender," she observed.

Don't dismiss me, I thought. *I'm so much more than an itinerant worker, going from job to job.*

My willingness to let things happen in their own time was fraying. I had that weak feeling in my knees again, and we hadn't even kissed. In the core of me an intense point of heat was growing. "Can we try the hot tub?" I said.

"Sure." Her eyes were dark, I hoped with desire.

We didn't touch as we stepped onto the veranda. Roanna had switched out the lights as we went outside, so our only illumination came from the rising moon pouring cold light from an inky sky.

The hot tub was bubbling quietly to itself. I stood beside it, looking at her. "We have to take our clothes off," she said, sounding amused.

I found my fingers were trembling. Ridiculous to feel this way, as though it were the first time I'd made love with a woman. She was already naked, and the moon shone along her flank, cast shadows under her breasts.

"Denise?" she said.

I realized I was still fully dressed, and felt abashed. "Sorry."

The water was tepid, and it fizzed against my skin like the champagne had in my mouth. Roanna sat opposite me, the water lapping her shoulders, her arms spread along the edge of the tub. "Tell me what you want," she said.

"You mean right now, or is this a whole-life question?"

"Either."

I treated her question seriously. "As far as my life is concerned, I want to do things that challenge me; I want to believe that I've achieved something." I fell silent, thinking how trite that sounded. "How about you?" I said.

Roanna didn't answer for a moment, then she said, "I want not to be unhappy."

"Are you unhappy?"

"Sometimes."

The hot tub burbled to itself, the faint scent rose from the water, my heart melted a little. I said, "Tell me what you want right now."

"To make love."

"That's excellent," I said, a tremor in my voice, "I feel the same way."

We met in the middle, buoyed by the bubbling water, filled with the same delightful purpose. "What do you like?" I whispered against her ear.

"Anything. Everything."

Her mouth was fire, I already knew that, but her bare wet skin against mine was incendiary. She touched my nipples, slid her hand down my stomach. "Roanna," I gasped.

"What?" she murmured.

"Just Roanna."

I was dissolving in the water, becoming pure sensation, but it wasn't enough. I wanted her under me, over me, her sweating skin sliding against mine. "You promised me your bed," I said.

"So I did."

We climbed out of the tub and went inside, our eyes so accustomed to the darkness that we needed no light. I had my arm around her, glorying in the length and strength of her, the way her ribs moved with her breathing.

Standing by the bed, locked together, the blood singing wildly in my ears, I felt every inhibition drop away. An alarm flared in my head. I had to hold fast to the fact that it was Denise Hunter making love to Roanna Aylmer, not me. Then she touched me and all thought melted away. I wanted her, and I wanted her never to stop.

We were on the bed, thrashing, abandoned. She arched beneath me, called out my name, once. Then she moaned, shrieked, and I rose up with her, flew with her. I was a skyrocket soaring, a shower of brilliant sparks.

"Pretty good," I said, panting, my face nestled into her throat.

She laughed through sobbing breath. "Oh please," she said. "Again."

CHAPTER TEN

I presented myself for work at the lounge the next morning a little bleary but inwardly singing with delight. The night was rolled up in my head like a wonderful gift that I'd always be able to open. We'd had breakfast together, then gone outside to drink our coffee with the singing birds and scented flowers. I could get to like this, a lot.

"You're not on this morning," said Jen, frowning at me from behind the bar. Even her red hair seemed indignant.

"Yes I am."

"You *were*." she said. "But there's been a change." It was obvious this was not to her liking. Her fair skin was flushed with annoyance. "I practically got no notice. It's not good enough!"

I was too tired to think straight this morning. "But why the change?" I said.

"You've been put on the catamaran with Pete to do drinks and catering. There's a cyclone warning out, so the trip to the reef for the conference people has been changed from tomorrow to today. You're supposed to be on board by eleven, so you'd better get a wriggle on."

That afternoon my contact, Alice, would arrive as a tourist taking a quick round trip to see the island. "I can't go," I said. "I'll have to swap with someone else."

"Don't even think of it," said Jen. "Harry Aylmer himself changed the roster to get you on the cat, so there's no way you can get off." She pursed her lips, considering me reflectively. "I've been wondering why."

I spread my hands. "I haven't the faintest idea."

Of course I had. I was betting it was my relationship with Roanna that had sparked his interest. Then a cold thought tickled my spine. What if the Aylmers were suspicious about me? What if it was intended that I be the next accident?

I apologized to Jen, as if it were all my fault, and left to consider my options. I decided that it was highly unlikely that the whole excursion was designed to provide an opportunity to eliminate me, so I went back to my original supposition that Harry had heard about his sister and me, and was planning to look me over. I could refuse to go on the catamaran, but that would certainly draw unfavorable attention from

Harry, and I didn't want to deal with his animosity, as it might isolate me from the family I was trying to investigate.

Okay. It was Plan B. I went back to the staff building to use one of the pay phones set in a row near the kitchen. I fed coins into its maw, dialed the number I'd memorized, and waited for it to be answered.

"Hello?" said a middle-aged voice.

"Mum, it's Denise."

We'd never met, but the woman said, "Darling! I'm so pleased to hear your voice. What's happening with you?"

We nattered on for a few moments about this and that, and then I said, "Mum, you know I said I'd take a couple of days off and fly home to see you? Well, something's come up, so I won't be making it quite yet."

The voice laughed indulgently. "Something or someone, darling?"

I laughed in turn. "I can't fool you. I have met someone nice."

I fed the phone more coins, we chatted a bit longer, then rang off affectionately. It was a conversation I'd never had with my own mother, but it wasn't hard to fake. I'd seen it dramatized a thousand times in movies or on television.

I felt more relaxed, knowing that my control would know that I couldn't make the contact this afternoon but that everything was okay with me. Alice would, if all went to plan, turn up tomorrow, and we'd exchange communications then.

* * * * *

121

It was yet another beautiful morning, and not too brassily hot. High up the sky was streaked by white strands of cloud, showing a high wind, but there was only a gentle breeze at sea level. The catamaran ferry rose and fell delicately at the dock, its white sides gleaming. *Moreen* was emblazoned in curling blue letters. With the image of Moreen Aylmer in mind, the name didn't suit the awkward grace of the cat.

The crew, and Pete and I, were all on well before our passengers arrived, to make sure that by the time they trooped down the dock there would be nothing left to do but usher them onto the cat and cast off. Tim came panting along, pulling a trolley loaded with diving equipment. As Pete had already loaded everything of ours, I helped Tim get his stuff on board.

"It's a pest," he said as we worked. "I've had a bunch of bloody reporters at the dive shop for the last hour, asking stupid questions about Lloyd Snead and his last dive. I told them at least a hundred times that I didn't supply the scuba gear to him, but it didn't make any difference."

"Where did Snead get the gear from?" I said. "What's your best guess?"

"I'm not sure," said Tim, "but there are at least a couple of guests who are really expert divers, and I remember Mr. Snead got talking to one of them a day or so before the accident."

"Oh yes?" I said, my tone as casual as possible. "I probably know the person from the bar. Who was it?"

"Tall woman. Cindy something. She's really friendly."

"Tanned like a leather shoe," I said.

Tim laughed. "That's the one."

I carted a couple more tanks on board, then said, "Did you tell the cops about Cindy talking to Snead?"

He looked at me with surprise. "Hell no. Why should I?"

Pete appeared on the deck. "Hey, you two, come aboard. We're all supposed to meet the captain and salute her." He grinned at our expressions. "She's traditional," he said.

I hadn't met the captain before. She was a smooth-faced woman whose white uniform was a little too tight for her ample body. She gave us a curt welcome when we were introduced, obviously in no mood to pay more than cursory attention to the hired help. She did bark orders in a satisfactory nautical fashion, however, and her minuscule crew — numbering only three — obeyed her with alacrity, so who was I to criticize?

Harry Aylmer, in dazzling white shorts and shirt that contrasted nicely with his heavy tan and black hair, came aboard with the guests. He was making an effort to be agreeable, listening attentively to remarks made to him and smiling and nodding at appropriate times.

The engines hummed, we moved from the dock, and within a few minutes we were scudding along, the cat high on its pontoons, leaving a bright white wake foaming behind us. The ocean was calm, the ride smooth, and everyone was in good spirits. I caught snatches of Indonesian, and words I recognized as Thai, but mostly people used the common language of English. Harry Aylmer circulated like a good host, but I was aware that he glanced over at me every so often.

The whole central portion of the catamaran was designed for hospitality and entertainment. Windows ran along each side, so that the area was filled with a delightful atmosphere of sunlight and salty air. Pete was kept busy behind the curved blue metal bar providing coffee and drinks, while I set out the buffet lunch on long tables built under the windows on the port side.

I knew that we would be on duty all day, and of course we couldn't join these important guests as they explored the coral reef, but memories of a treasured holiday when I was twelve, the last I had with my mother before she died, reminded me of what they would be seeing.

Mum and I had visited a section of the Great Barrier Reef near Cairns, and I could still recall my excitement as I had placed the mouthpiece of the snorkel in my mouth and positioned my face mask. Underwater a whole world of color and movement met my enchanted eyes. The memories of that wonderful time combined to form a cascade of brilliant images: delicate coral, pink and yellow; blue starfish; red anemones waving fragile tentacles; parrotfish and angelfish and butterfly cod; gracefully creepy manta rays flapping past; schools of tiny, iridescent fishes, darting together in a ballet of precise movements; crabs and sea slugs, sea urchins, giant clams.

I started as Pete clapped me on the shoulder. "You daydreaming again?"

"Again? When have I done it before?"

"When you're dreaming of Roanna," he said with a wicked smile.

I felt myself blush. With the undoubted efficiency of the gossip machine on the island, the fact that I'd spent the entire night with her would probably be common knowledge by the time we got back.

Luncheon was announced, and the captain and guests descended on the laden table. The food was similar to that served at the Aylmers' function, with an emphasis on fresh shellfish of all kinds, plus a wide variety of salad dishes. I'd warmed bread in the galley's oven, and its yeasty scent made my mouth water. Pete, Tim and I couldn't eat until the conference attendees had finished, and the crew had taken a turn.

I hovered near the table, tidying, rearranging and rushing off to get more bread when required. Farid Sabir had his bodyguards close by him even here, although I couldn't imagine what they thought could happen on the catamaran with a crowd of potential witnesses and no way to escape. *Unless*, I thought with a wry smile, *someone suggested skeet shooting.*

In photographs I'd seen of Sabir he'd looked like a weedy little nonentity, but in real life he was far more impressive, having a deep voice, a penetrating gaze and a quick smile.

One of his bodyguards, a solid guy almost as wide as he was tall, frisked me with his eyes, lingering on my breasts, then gave me a gap-toothed smile. He went back to read my name tag, sounding *Denise* silently to himself. Yuck! I escaped his further attention by going behind the bar to help Pete with coffee. I was putting out cups and saucers, and had just got into a pleasant rhythm, when Harry Aylmer came over. He nodded to Pete, and said to me, "Denise, I'd like a word with you."

He pointed to the small deck to the rear of the cabin. "Out there."

There was no one near us, and I had a vision of Harry picking me up and tossing me over the stern. I was a strong swimmer, so maybe I could eventually make it to land, that is, if a shark didn't get me.

He interrupted this fancy by saying, "You've become friendly with my sister." The stiff breeze whipped his dark hair, and gave him a not entirely unpleasant devil-may-care air.

I'd decided to respond to him with an obliging, but reserved, manner. "Yes, I have."

"I wouldn't want you to take it too seriously."

"I won't."

He looked at me sharply. "There have been a lot before you, and there'll be a lot after."

"That's fine. I get bored with one place, and move on."

He nodded. Obviously I'd said what he wanted to hear. "Good, then we understand each other."

"I think so."

Harry gave me a satisfied smile, one that made we want to king-hit him right on his arrogant nose. That he was a blood relative to the woman whom I'd held in my arms all night was almost too incredible to believe. I looked at his face, seeing a slight resemblance to Roanna in the line of his eyebrows and the set of his jaw. "May I go back?" I said.

"Of course." He patted me on the shoulder, and I only just stopped myself from recoiling. "Good," he said. "Good."

Tim bolted down lunch while the crew anchored the cat near the section of the reef that best displayed its underwater glories. For those who preferred a less adventurous viewing of the coral and reef creatures, there was a small boat with a glass insert in the bottom. I wished I could go out in that, and look down like a god at massive corals of purple and brown, delicate branching corals in pastel shades, red crabs and fat urchins and brittle stars. And the gaudy tropical fish, startling in the variety of their colors and shapes.

Pete and I ate a late lunch in the galley. Even after the enthusiastic appetites that had preceded us, there was still plenty of choice, although to my regret I found all the bread had disappeared.

"Jen said something about a cyclone warning," I said.

Pete chewed, swallowed. "Why do you always ask questions when I've got a mouthful?"

"Just good timing, I guess."

That got him grinning again. "I bet that was handy last night."

"Pete."

He put up his hands. "Okay, okay. The subject's off limits. About the cyclone, there's one way out the Pacific, but it could head this way. If it does, it'll probably blow itself out and just be a tropical storm, but I'd say we're in for a lot of rain. The weather bureau has named it Anthony. You know anyone called Anthony?"

It so happened that I did. My only serious fling at being heterosexual had been with an Anthony when I was in my late teens. I'd been very organized about the whole thing and had really given it my best shot, but going to bed with Anthony had produced no storm, no thunder and lightning, merely a conviction that it wasn't the way I was going to go. I remembered that Anthony was quite pleased with our encounter, but I found it a total waste of time, and said so, tact not being my strong point at that stage.

"I knew an Anthony once," I said. "He married my best friend and became a politician."

"Lucky escape for you," said Pete. "Those pollies can be the pits."

Once we had organized the light refreshments that would sustain the guests on the way back to the island, there was nothing for us to do. I wandered out onto the narrow deck that ran right around the main body of the vessel. It was low tide, and fifty meters away several people were walking the exposed reef itself. Closer to the cat, heads were bobbing in the water and Tim was doing his best to teach novices the basics of snorkeling before they plunged down to view the wonders of the reef. A few, obviously expert, flipped under the water with scuba tanks attached. I saw Harry Aylmer's black head, and realized he was one of them.

Now that I had time to process what Tim had told me, I tried to visualize every time I'd seen Cynthia Urquhart. At first when he'd mentioned her name I'd been astonished to think she might have anything to do with Snead's death, but now I thought of her strong, wiry build, and I had no trouble seeing her wrench the mouthpiece from Snead's lips and then get behind him, holding it out of his clutching fingers, until asphyxia forced him to take an agonizing lungful of water.

I found I was holding my own breath, and let it out in a long sigh. Drowning was supposed to be a great way to die, but I couldn't believe that was true. My thoughts kept skipping from scenario to scenario.

Maybe Cindy had nothing to do with it — Harry Aylmer was at home with scuba gear, so maybe he had drowned Snead.

Or perhaps someone had tampered with the tanks Snead wore, so that he was breathing, say, carbon monoxide. Then he'd slide into unconsciousness without anyone being anywhere near him, lose his mouthpiece, and breathe in water without even feeling it sear his lungs.

Jeez! I was holding my breath again.

I looked up at the sky, searching for some sign that Cyclone Anthony was on his way to batter our island paradise. There were clouds on the horizon, but above the sky was a clear, pale blue. The breeze had picked up even more, however, and little whitecaps were flicking foam into the air. There were no big breakers here, of course. To the east of us the full might of the Pacific was beating itself to nothing against the ramparts of the outer Barrier Reef. Only in a powerful storm would the water enclosed by the reef have high seas.

The catamaran set off for home in late afternoon. The clouds had grown heavier and darker, and before we reached the island the sun had been blotted out.

"There's a blow coming," said Pete, with the attitude of a master mariner.

Tim laughed at him. "You only know that, mate, because you've heard a weather forecast."

"Mark my words," said Pete, "it's going to be a big one."

I thought Pete might be right, as whitecaps were rolling in the normally placid sea inside the reef's protection. The catamaran still scooted along, cutting through the wave tops with exhilarating ease. The passengers were subdued, most of them sitting and talking quietly, but the smooth ride ensured that no one, including me, showed any sign of seasickness.

As a kid, I could vividly remember rough weather on my uncle's fishing boat, and me leaning over the side to throw up while my brother, who had an iron stomach, jeered at my weakness. I understood very well the old joke: *When you get seasick, first you worry you'll die. Then you worry you won't!*

My heart leapt when we approached the dock. Roanna was waiting there, leaning against the white railing, her hair blowing across her face.

"I'll look after everything," said Pete. "You go on ahead."

I waited until the other passengers had disembarked, not as smooth a procedure as in the morning, as now the cat bucked and pitched in the rising sea. I leapt, gracefully I hoped, onto the dock. "Hey," I said.

"Hey, yourself."

A sudden gust of wind buffeted us. She flung her head back to look at the sky, which was wild with torn clouds. Lightning flickered on the horizon. "It's going to pour. You've heard there's a cyclone warning?"

"Sounds exciting."

She leaned close to me to say softly, "I love making love in a storm."

My body responded as if a button had been pressed. "Me too," I said.

Roanna looked past me toward the cat, and her expression changed. I turned to see her brother standing on the narrow deck. Roanna said, her voice icy, "Hello, Harry."

"Ro."

I looked from one to the other. The tension was palpable, as though unspoken acid words were vibrating in the air.

Roanna took my arm. "Come on."

I imagined I could feel the heat of Harry's stare like a laser beam between my shoulder blades. "What's going on?"

"Nothing." She looked across at me. "Harry has warned you off, I imagine." Her voice was hard with fury.

"Not exactly."

She stopped to face me. "What does that mean?"

"He told me there'd been lots before me, and would be lots after me."

She was sardonic. "And that I'd break your heart?"

"He didn't mention that," I said, "but there's a fair chance that you could."

CHAPTER ELEVEN

There'd been a computer glitch of some sort in the convention center, and it had to be fixed for tomorrow's conference sessions, so Roanna had to go back to work. "I don't know how long I'll be," she said.

The disappointment was like a slap. "I probably need an early night," I said.

Her lips twitched. "Sounds good to me." She handed me a plastic card. "This opens the main security gate. I won't be any later than nine, I hope.

The house is unlocked, so why don't you go there when you're ready, have something to eat, take a shower, and I'll join you as soon as I can."

"I've got my reputation to think of," I said. "I don't want you to think I'm easy." I looked at her mouth. "There are worse things to be. Give me the keycard."

Jen's room was down the hall from mine, and I bumped into her on my way to collect a change of clothes. "Hi," I said, not slowing. I wanted to be in Roanna's house, smelling her scent, glancing at her books.

"Den, I wonder if we could talk."

I looked at Jen more closely, realizing with a jolt that her eyes were swollen from crying. She gave a little tearful hiccup. "Please, Den."

How could I resist an appeal like this? "Your room or mine?" I said, thinking wryly that Jen and I, thanks to our affairs with Aylmer siblings, would be the most likely to have our bedrooms bugged, if indeed bugging was going on.

"Mine's closer," she sniffed.

Her room was standard issue, just like mine. The furniture was the same; the ubiquitous beige was everywhere, although Jen had a brightly colored rug to break the monotony, and I noted that her ceiling fan looked less geriatric than the dinosaur I had.

I checked the books and magazines she had on her bedside table, working on the principle that a great deal can be learned from what a person reads. Jen had a bodice-ripper romance and a self-help titled

When Your Man Doesn't Listen. The magazines covered fashion and entertainment.

Jen snatched a tissue from a box and blew her nose, hard. She plucked out four more, folding them into a wad, and dabbed forlornly at her cheeks. Perching on the edge of the bed, she gestured me to the beige plastic chair by the desk.

Apart from some aberrant people, generally film stars, heavy crying is guaranteed to make a person look unappealing. Jen, unfortunately, was one who looked positively diseased. Her face was blotched in various intensities of red, her nose rivaled Rudolf's, and the whites of her eyes had turned an extraordinary pink.

"Jen, what has upset you?" I said, sympathy and inquiry nicely blended.

"It's Quint." She waved one skinny white arm around in a furious gesture. "I could just kill him, Den! Really I could."

"That's awful," I said, "What's he done?"

My question brought a new flood of tears. Through the wad of tissues I could just decipher, ". . . and he *promised.*"

"Promised what?"

Making a brave attempt at composure, Jen straightened her shoulders. Clearing her throat, she said, "We had these plans. Quint promised he'd take a couple of days off, so I went ahead and swapped around shifts so I'd be covered. We were going to fly to the mainland tonight, and stay at the very best hotel and go shopping and all that. It was going to be lovely, spending all that time together." Her lips trembled.

I supposed that Quint's mother, or Harry, perhaps,

had heard of Quint's plans and put a kibosh on them. "What went wrong?"

Jen's face was flushed, but now it was anger coming to the fore. "The trouble is, I'm not important enough to him. If Quint *really* cared for me, he wouldn't let some stupid business meeting get in the way." She looked to me for support. "Would he?"

I was interested in any business meeting the Aylmers might have. "That's a bloody shame," I said with a touch of indignation on Jen's behalf. "You shouldn't be treated that way."

She was definitely angry now. "I should have stood up for myself, not got upset when he told me we couldn't go."

"What reason did he give?"

She shook her head impatiently. "Someone's coming here today. It's all a big secret, but Quint had to boast about it." With a flash of insight, she added, "You know, he does like to big-note himself. It was like he was in on something important, and he couldn't not tell me about it."

"So who is this mysterious person?"

"I never really found out. Quint said something about a wolf, a red wolf. I wasn't paying that much attention, because I was trying not to cry."

I said a soothing word or two, but my heart was jumping in my chest. Red Wolf. The code name for an international terrorist who had bombed buildings and assassinated key players for the past fifteen years. His real name had never been established, and there was only one known fuzzy photograph of his face. He'd never even come close to being caught.

I needed more confirmation than this. "Are you sure Quint mentioned a red wolf?"

"I think so. I wasn't paying much attention. Quint said it was a big secret, and he made me promise not to tell anyone." She gave me a watery smile, "Well, whoops! I've gone and told you, Den."

"Don't give it another thought," I said.

I couldn't wait until the contact with Alice tomorrow, so I went straight to the bank of pay phones near the rec room. There were people around, but even if someone overheard me, I had to break silence, whatever the risk, if there was any possibility Red Wolf was coming to the resort. I had to take into account that the phones might be tapped, so it was obvious I'd blow it if I used the terrorist's name.

When the call picked up I knew that I'd be automatically recorded, and I would use a code of phrases that at least would indicate there was a most-wanted was on the island. That wasn't good enough, so I was vainly trying to work out how I could get some subtle reference into the conversation that would alert ASIO to the name Red Wolf. Ludicrous possibilities that I might weave into the conversation popped into my mind: ruddy dog, russet canine, a wolf in a scarlet sheep's clothing, keeping the carmine wolf from the door.

I was clearly getting hysterical, but with very good reason. If I came right out and said Red Wolf and the telephone were tapped, then he'd be long gone and there was a good possibility I would be too.

The first phone I tried had no dial tone, and I was about to try the second when Seb turned up with an OUT OF ORDER sign. "Bad luck, Den. All the phones are dead on the island. Some problem with the exchange on the mainland."

Hell! "Have you got a mobile phone?"

"It's hard, but I'm living without one," he said sardonically. Perhaps my anxiety showed, because he added, "That must be some important call."

"Not really."

I left him hanging the sign and went back to my room, ticking off my options. Find someone with a mobile and borrow it seemed the best way to go. Then inspiration struck: Roanna's computer was linked by satellite to the Internet, and she wasn't home. I'd seen her use her password, so I could log on and send an e-mail message to several key people at once. All that boring time spent memorizing contact information was about to pay off.

I grabbed a change of clothes and my toothbrush and toilet bag, thinking how much I wished I had a gun. I checked my watch. After seven. I'd really have to move. I opened my door and came face to face with Seb.

"Hi, again," he said. His substantial body blocked the way, so I would have to push past him to get out.

I was in a hurry, but suddenly it didn't seem wise to make that obvious. "Seb," I said with a smile. "What a pleasure to see you twice in ten minutes."

He looked at my shoulder bag. "And where are you off to?"

"To sell my body on the street," I announced. "Not that there's much of a street available, but I thought I'd lurk near the Jitterbug and hope for the best."

"Good luck," he said, laughing.

When he didn't move, I said, "And I can help you with . . . ?"

137

Seb ran his hand over his sandy hair, so awkwardly guileless that I was immediately suspicious. Not *Seb*. Surely, of all people, I could trust him to be what he appeared to be.

"I was thinking, Den," he said, "that lots of the guests have mobile phones. If it's a really important call, I'll ask around and borrow one for you."

Oscar Fallon. In my panic I hadn't thought of Fallon before. It went against the grain to go for help to the CIA, but if this wasn't an emergency, what was? "Great idea, Seb. I remember one of the guests has a cell phone, and I'm quite friendly with him."

"Who is it?"

His face was still Seb's, open and honest, but I couldn't fully trust him, or anyone else, for that matter. "Oscar Fallon," I said, taking a chance on Seb because if he helped me find the CIA guy, I could get the alarm out that much faster.

"Jeez, Den, you're out of luck again. Mr. Fallon's left the island. I know because I took his luggage to the plane."

"Hey," I said, throwing up my hands, "It was a guilt trip, anyway. My mum was expecting me to spend some time with her, but I dipped out, and I know she's upset about it."

I heard my trainer's ghostly voice: *Don't get too complicated*.

"You know how it is," I went on, "mothers have this built-in talent to make you feel bad. Probably better I don't ring. It'd just give her more ammunition."

"So you're not going to make the call?"

"No point really."

Seb stepped aside to let me out into the hallway.

As I passed him he put an arm around me and gave me a hard squeeze. "Look after yourself," he said.

My thoughts kept time with my brisk footsteps. If Red Wolf had come to the island, I was faced with a career highlight . . . or a total disaster. And why would the terrorist be on Aylmer Island?

My mind zipped through the background briefings I'd had on the Aylmer family's suspected activities. It was a range of national security nightmares: sophisticated identity fraud, money laundering; the provision of cutting-edge financial and technological information to international radicals and activists.

For a long time the conventions the resort featured had been under investigation, but evidence of criminal activities that would stand up in court was difficult to find. The Aylmers hosted genuine conferences, organized for reputable companies and organizations, but there were also invitation-only meetings that catered to powerful people — politicians, financiers, political heavyweights.

Murder-for-hire had not featured in the prospectus, at least not until recently. Bellamy's death, and then Snead's drowning, seemed to indicate this policy had changed. Was Farid Sabir the next victim?

It didn't seem a big enough project to tempt Red Wolf. Bodyguards or not, the assassination of a political leader was not so difficult, as witness the parade of deaths in the last decades. Something else, then . . .

What sort of target would be worth the attention of the very top entrepreneur of terrorism? A key figure, someone whose death would have momentous consequences. What vital world figure was visiting Australia at the moment? Hell, I should have paid more attention to the cascade of memos that crossed my desk.

Eerie blue light flickered, followed almost immediately by the ear-splitting crack of thunder. I'd been so caught up in my thoughts I'd hardly noticed the worsening weather. A splatter of rain hit my face. It wasn't cold, but the wind had intensified until the palms fronds thrashed.

Stopping at the bottom of the drive that led to the compound, I considered the fact that once I walked around the first curve I'd be in the view of the surveillance cameras. What to do? I didn't want to be seen going in, but the keycard Roanna had given me opened that gate at the top of the drive.

I turned the plain plastic rectangle over in my fingers. On Roanna's private path to the ocean there was a steel security gate. But no camera that I could remember. It was logical to assume that this key fitted that gate too.

I'd take a chance it did. The rain was falling harder, great fat drops that set up spurts of dust where they hit the ground. I checked my watch again. Nearly eight. I broke into a jog. This was going to be close.

CHAPTER TWELVE

By the time I'd reached the security gate below Roanna's place, the storm had achieved a frightening intensity. Lit by bolts of lightning, purple-black clouds boiled overhead, and the shrieking wind was bending coconut palms as though they were insubstantial stems of grass. Rain, blown almost horizontal, stung my face.

I fumbled with the keycard, knowing that every moment was precious, and if I had to go back to the main gate I might not have time to send a message before Roanna came home. The keycard worked.

Caught by the wind, the gate slammed open. I fought to close it behind me. The storm was like a thinking thing, a huge malicious force that wanted to thrash air, water and land into subjugation.

I stumbled up the path, branches lashing at me as if I were running a gauntlet of enraged vegetation. Roanna had left the outside lights on, and they winked at me like beacons through the tumult. I skirted the veranda, which was covered with shredded leaves, and made it to the front door. It was unlocked.

Inside, the comparative quiet was startling. I was soaked to the skin, and a puddle of water was rapidly forming where I stood. I called out Roanna's name, sure that she wasn't there, but feeling, suddenly, like an intruder who was about to betray her trust. No time to change. I took off my wet sneakers and left them by the front door, then I grabbed a towel from the bathroom and dried myself off so I wouldn't track water wherever I went. Roughly toweling my dripping hair, I went from room to room, double-checking that I was alone.

Looking out the streaming window toward the Big House, I could see lights lining the pathway as a confused pattern of dots that appeared and disappeared through the lashing branches. No Roanna. No Harry or Quint hurrying down to ask me what the hell I thought I was doing.

The computer was on, the monitor resting. The screen sprang to life as soon as I touched the mouse, glowing with warmth, with reassurance. I slid onto the seat and guided the cursor. Outside a ferocious blast seemed about to smash into the room. I looked over my shoulder. In all this racket I'd never hear someone behind me.

Was the satellite dish secure? The storm was fierce enough to tear it up and send it, wires trailing, into the air. Or perhaps Harry and Quint, pliers in hand, were just about to sever the connection.

It wasn't cold, but I was shivering. I called up Roanna's Internet provider, keyed in her password, *Roanna,* and watched the screen change. She had mail: I didn't care. I hit the *Send Message* command.

I'd been so intent on getting there, that I'd hardly thought what I would write. What about, *Help! Red Wolf is here and I can't cope.* True, but not what a cool, professional agent would send.

In the *Send to* box I filled in the ASIO control, as well as every ASIO person I could think of, with no attempt to put them in order of superiority. This was no time to worry about hurt feelings. I stared at the spot where the cursor blinked at the beginning of the heading line. *Extreme Violation* I typed. It wasn't entirely accurate, but would get immediate attention, as it indicated there had been a fatal security breach.

Branches rattled at the window. My breath caught in my throat as something skittered across the veranda — a branch, a palm frond. It could have been a person, and I was wasting time trying to compose the perfect message.

Most urgent advice: Bed Wolf, I typed. I groaned. Obviously a Freudian slip. I corrected it to *Red.* Okay, be brief and to the point.

Most urgent advice: Red Wolf on Aylmer Island as guest in Aylmer house. Repeat, Red Wolf. Potential of positive ID high. Imperative extreme urgent action initiated. Subject may leave at any time. This channel NOT secure. Do NOT reply to this e-mail.

I signed it with my code name, which changed at

midnight every day. *Gypsum*. Tomorrow it would be *Silica*.

Sitting in my wet clothes, I shuddered. I hit *Send*. After one long moment, the screen declared, *Message Sent*.

I let out my breath in a long sigh, then did it all again. The second time I remembered another e-mail address to add — naturally someone who'd be slighted to note he wasn't in the first group — headed the message *Backup Notification,* worded it differently, in case there was any ambiguity I hadn't detected in the first one, and sent it up to the satellite riding silent space high above the storm.

Hunching my shoulders as though some intruder had entered and was poised behind me, I pulled up *Sent Messages* and deleted any record that my e-mails had been electronically mailed. I quickly scanned the messages that Roanna had sent and received. Nothing jumped out at me. I looked over my shoulder. No one was there.

I had more to do before Roanna returned: Mop up the wet chair, the floor, so that there'd no sign I'd been at the computer; do a quick search of the desk, the filing cabinets; change into dry clothes; look for a gun. I had to have a weapon . . .

I was shivering so hard my teeth were chattering. Clothes first. I'd just put on faded jeans and was pulling one of Roanna's T-shirts over my head as I came into the main room when the front door was flung open.

"Jesus Christ!" said Roanna, blown in by a savage blast of wet air. "It's bloody wet out there."

She shook herself like a dog, splattering the surrounding area with droplets, smiled at me, and with one stride had grabbed me and kissed me. Sex, love, were impossible to think of while an international terrorist was only a short walk away up the hill. My mind was quite clear on that point. My body wasn't. My lips opened under her hard kiss.

After all, I thought fuzzily, what was there for me to do? ASIO would advise the nearest authorities, including the military; special support groups would be mobilized; airports would be monitored; and, if any vessels could brave the storm, the coast guard would set up a cordon around the island.

So what could Denise Cleever, undercover agent, actually do? Not a thing, except take this gorgeous woman to bed and wait for the cavalry to ride to the rescue.

"I'm starving," said Roanna. "How about scrambled eggs?"

Immediately my mouth watered. "Terrific. I'll do them while you get changed."

While she was in the bedroom I slipped into the computer alcove and mopped the floor and chair. Outside, the wind howled even louder, and rain hit the window near me with the force of flung pebbles.

I was back in the kitchen when Roanna came out, brushing her hair. "This storm's going to put a dent in the President's plans," she said.

I stopped beating the eggs. "President of what?"

"Don't you keep up with the news? President of the good ole US of A."

I must have gaped at her, because she laughed and said, "It's a lightning trip. He's been in New Zealand for a Pacific nations economic summit, and instead of flying home, he's changed his plans to include a quick visit to Australia, namely the Daintree Rain Forest."

This wasn't far from Aylmer Island. "Where is he now?" I said.

Roanna raised her eyebrows at my urgent tone. "I didn't realize you were a fan."

"Just a bit interested."

"Can't help you much. Maybe the whole plan's been abandoned, although the forecast is that the storm should blow itself out."

"Oh yeah?" I said, as a fresh assault shook the house.

"If you like, we can pick up the news." She flicked on the television. "We get a zillion channels through the dish."

"Please make the toast," I said, trying to keep an eye on the television headline news whilst pouring the beaten eggs into a pan.

The American President's visit was the third story. He was shown playing golf in the rain with selected Aussie politicians, grinning cheerfully whilst his grim bodyguards trudged the course looking wet and unhappy. The effervescent voice of the announcer burbled on about the President's obsession with golf and how he was determined not to let the vagaries of weather stop any of his plans. In fact, she added with admiring warmth, his outing to the Daintree Rain Forest with the Prime Minister would go ahead, even if it was still raining heavily.

The lights flickered, then steadied. Roanna smiled across at me. "The power could go out, but don't worry — I'm sure we'll find something to do in the dark."

I smiled in turn, but my thoughts were buzzing about something entirely different. Of course ASIO would put two and two together and realize that the

President would be Red Wolf's primary target. I reassured myself that security for any leading politician, even in a safe country like Australia, would be very tight, anyway, but in my mind's eye I could see the last political assassination Red Wolf had engineered. It had been logistically and technically a masterpiece, and along with the intended victims, the bomb had killed over fifty bystanders.

It didn't have to be a bomb. This international terrorist had used any number of different techniques, and he had always overseen the hit itself, then escaped like smoke into the air.

"If you don't stir that," Roanna admonished me, indicating the pan on the stove, "we're going to have a fat, shapeless omelet instead of scrambled eggs."

"Sorry."

I didn't hear the door open, just felt the wet blast of air. I turned around, pan in one hand, wooden spoon in the other. My heart jumped sharply.

"Hello girls," said Eddie Trebonus. The gun he held was very familiar to me. A snub-nosed, double-action Smith & Wesson .38 automatic. Practical, deadly, and efficient.

CHAPTER THIRTEEN

Eddie Trebonus closed the door behind him. Water glistened on his face, and his flabby body was swathed in an outsize black raincoat from which water streamed onto the floor.

The gun was pointed at me, not Roanna. I glanced at her. She looked astonished, and then anger took over. "What the hell do you think you're doing, Eddie? What is this? The Wild West? Put the gun away."

I measured this distance between Eddie and me. The breakfast bar was between us, so I had to get around it to have a clear path to him. Putting down the pan and spoon, and having the presence of mind to turn off the gas, I quavered, "I don't understand."

"Of course you do, Den." He was swollen with power and arrogance. "You understand perfectly."

Okay, how would Denise Hunter act now? I moved a little farther toward the end of the breakfast bar. To Roanna I said, "He won't hurt us, will he?"

"Not if he wants to continue living," Roanna ground out.

It was important for me to appear helpless, weak. Eddie had to be off guard, if only for a moment. Tears would have been a help, but my eyes were resolutely dry. Besides, something in me rebelled at crying or pleading, and also I had to admit that I didn't want to look a total wimp in front of Roanna.

I took another step. "Please, Mr. Trebonus, you're frightening me," I said.

"You're not frightening me, Eddie, you stupid bastard." Roanna's voice cracked like a whip. "Get out of here before I call my mother, and this really gets out of hand."

He was amused. "It was your mother who sent me," he said. His attention switched to me. "Now, Den, I can be nasty or nice. All depends on you."

Denise Hunter, if she existed, wouldn't be able to believe what was happening to her. "I can't believe this," I said. "What have I ever done to you, Mr. Trebonus?"

His thick lips split in a smile. "Oh, honey, you can call me Eddie." His wet shoes squished as he took a step in my direction. "We're going to get to know each other very well before the night is out."

"This has gone far enough." Roanna was flushed with rage. "Get out of my house."

149

"No deal. Now shut up, Ro, or I'll have to get rough with you."

There were two of us against him, and if Roanna had had the right training, we could work in tandem and probably disarm him without anyone being hurt. As it was, I presumed she knew little about self-defense, so she would be a liability if I made a move on Eddie because I couldn't be sure how she'd react.

I'd chance it. I couldn't be sure Eddie would remain alone, and the odds would most certainly be against me if he had backup. I took a deep breath. In the gym, disarming exercises were quite fun, but now the whole maneuver had a desperate edge that made my stomach flutter and my hands sweat.

"This is too bloody much!" Roanna moved toward Eddie, as if she were about to demand he hand over his weapon.

The sound of the shot was absolutely deafening. My ears rang as though my head was a bell that had been hit by a hammer. Eddie had fired into the floor, and Roanna seemed frozen in mid step.

I whimpered and put my hands to my face. "Don't hurt us," I cried, my voice tremulous. "We'll do whatever you say."

I was around the breakfast bar now. A couple of strides, and he'd be mine. His throat, his eyes, his balls. Rage was tightening my muscles, flowing like fire through my veins.

"Eddie, this is insane."

"Shut up, Ro."

Get him talking. What a cliché that was, but like all clichés it held an element of truth. "What is it you think I've done?" I asked, clasping my hands. "This has got to be some dreadful mistake. Just tell me what it is. What am I supposed to have done?"

Eddie's pleased expression showed how much he enjoyed the note of supplication in my voice.

"We had our suspicions from the start," he said grandly. "You made mistakes."

"Mistakes about what? I don't understand."

Eddie shifted his stance slightly, getting comfortable so he could deliver an explanation of why he was so clever, and I was so dumb.

"Your first big mistake was contacting Oscar Fallon."

I was genuinely dumbfounded. I hadn't known the guy was CIA. I'd spoken to him by chance. "Who?" I said.

"Don't pretend you don't know he's a CIA agent."

Looking bewildered, I said, "CIA?" My voice rose on the last letter to add to the impression of stupefaction.

Roanna looked at me, then back to Eddie. "What's this about?"

"On the beach," said Eddie, "you thought it looked like a little chat to a stranger, didn't you? Well, we were watching." He gave a self-satisfied grunt. "Fallon's up at the Big House, and he'll talk, like you will, with the right persuasion."

"Jesus," said Roanna, "this is like a bad movie."

"Shut the hell up, Ro. I mean it."

He had relaxed a little, thought of himself as being in control of two weak women. Ready, steady . . .

The door crashed open. Quint stood there, his yellow slicker dripping, his wet hair plastered to his skull. In his hands he held a double-barreled shotgun. I felt a hysterical giggle stall in my throat. This *was* like a bad movie.

"Fuck it, Eddie," snarled Quint, "I might have known you couldn't pull it off by yourself." He glared at Roanna. "You and your fucking girlfriends. Mum's warned you before."

He gestured to me with the shotgun. "Up to the Big House, quick smart, and don't give me any trouble or I'll blow you away." He aimed a tight-lipped smile at Roanna. "You, too, Sis."

"And if I don't, you'll shoot me?" Roanna's tone was incredulous.

"Shoot you? Hell no. But I'll smash your face in if I have to. This isn't a game, Ro. Get moving."

With Quint's arrival, Eddie had shrunk to second banana. The automatic drooped in his hand, and his expression was disconsolate. I thought seriously of going for his gun, but Quint was watching me, mean-eyed, the light glinting on the long barrel of the shotgun. I had a flash of a hot sunny day skeet shooting, and Morrie Bellamy falling, his cranium shattered.

Quint said to me, "You first, and don't try making a run for it, because it'll be the last thing you do."

I believed him. He was edgy, excited, as if holding a woman at the point of a gun was a charge. I waited until the door was open and the rain was swirling into the room before I spoke. "It's raining," I said, as though avoiding a drenching was the most important issue of the moment.

"Get going."

I was barefoot, and the ground outside was littered with debris from the storm. If any opportunity occurred to escape in the darkness, I needed shoes on my feet. Indicating my wet sneakers beside the front door, I said with a mulish note in my voice, "I want to put my shoes on first."

Quint gave an irritated grunt. "Hurry up," he said.

The sneakers were cold and heavy with water. I laced them on with clumsy fingers, then Quint shoved me out into the storm. I went first up the pathway, Quint jabbing the shotgun into my back every few steps. I screwed up my eyes as the rain, blown by the weight of the wind, peppered my face like a blast of sand. Glancing back, I could see Roanna had fallen in after her brother, with Eddie bringing up the rear.

If anyone spoke, I didn't hear it. The storm was ferocious, a continuous wet roar that seemed to shake the ground. My mind was running scenarios as I stumbled up the path: make a wild break for it now and hope for the best; go along with it all and confess; play dumb to the end; plead with Moreen Aylmer for my release; threaten them that ASIO would not rest until they were arrested.

ASIO would realize that something had happened to me when I didn't make the contact with Alice tomorrow. Right now, no one knew I was a prisoner, and even if that were known, the capture of Red Wolf would have priority.

A branch slashed my cheek. I was totally soaked, my jeans and T-shirt sticking to me like a second skin, and Roanna, who had no protection either, must be as miserable as I was. I trudged up the incline, the shotgun smashing into my ribs at regular intervals, hating the whole experience, yet not anxious to get to the Big House, where I was fearful some terrible experience awaited me.

We came through a side entrance into the central courtyard, and the noise of the storm immediately dropped to a manageable clamor. The courtyard was streaming with water, the dolphin fountain blurred by gray sheets of falling rain. It was nothing like Saturday's scene. If only I could be there again, with the soft music, people talking and laughing, the soft wind blowing, and Roanna in that black dress, poised, enigmatic, infinitely desirable.

I turned my head to see her. She stared back at me, bedraggled but glowing with fury. "I'll sort it all out," she said to me. "Don't worry."

Quint laughed. "Sure, Ro. You always get what you want, don't you?"

"What I want is simple. That you get the hell out of my life."

Quint narrowed his eyes at her. "Harry wants to see you." He jerked his head at Eddie. "Take her. I'll look after this other bitch." He indicated a door to me. "In there."

I obeyed, keeping my body language full of fear. "Please don't hurt me."

We were in a wide and thickly carpeted corridor, hushed after the racket outside. Paintings, each carefully lit, lined the walls. There was the smell of money, of privilege, in the air-conditioned air.

Moreen Aylmer was waiting for us in a room for which the word *elegant* was far too gross. The walls were ivory, the carpet white, the pale furniture so finely drawn it seemed insubstantial. I took a small pleasure that I was dripping water in this pristine place.

"Denise," she said, as though welcoming a guest. "Come in."

"There's been some mistake," I said in a trembling voice, gesturing toward Quint and the shotgun. "I haven't done anything wrong."

A shadow crossed her face. "Is that gun really necessary, dear?"

"Yes, Mother, it is."

She lifted her shoulders in a well-bred shrug. "Very well." Her attention came back to me. "I'm afraid you've been very foolish, Denise, if that is your name."

I looked confused. "Of course it's my name. What else would it be?"

Quint snorted. "She'll lie, of course. Let me do something to help her remember the truth."

Moreen put up a restraining hand. "I'm sure that won't be necessary. When Denise realizes that there's no point in putting up a front any more, I'm sure she'll cooperate."

"I've no idea what you're talking about." I leaked a note of panic into my voice. "I haven't done anything. Let me go! Please!"

The only effect of this was to make Moreen click her tongue in a ladylike way, although her eyes were hard as stone. "Perhaps it will help if you know that your conversation was recorded." When I looked blank, she went on, "Your conversation with that employee . . ."

"Jen," snapped Quint. "She's got a name. It's Jen."

Irrelevantly, I thought how delighted Jen would be if she knew that Quint was keen to have his mother show respect, even in Jen's absence.

"With that employee," Moreen repeated, her emphasis on the last word. Her lips tightened. "Quint, if you hadn't told the young woman sensitive information, this never would have happened. I hold you entirely responsible."

"Christ!" He swung the shotgun like a huge and deadly pointer, until it was centered on my face. "Don't blame *me*. This bitch was the one asking the questions, snooping around."

"Yes," said Moreen. She examined me as though I were a loathsome creature that had just crawled out from under a rock. "You've caused a great deal of trouble for yourself, my dear. First a contact with the CIA plant, then all those questions of staff members like little Vera, and then your attempts to insinuate yourself into my family. That I cannot forgive."

"Are you all insane?" I asked, not in anger, but in distress. "Please let me go. I'll forget it ever happened. Promise."

It was as if I hadn't spoken. "It's unforgivable that you should seduce Roanna."

I was sick of this. "Why?" I said.

"What do you know of Red Wolf?" asked Moreen Aylmer. At that moment I knew for sure that she didn't intend I get out of this alive. She had used the terrorist's name, and even Denise Hunter, innocent of any spying, would remember the question and repeat it. With a chill I realized that it didn't matter to them if I were tortured now, since I would be eliminated after they'd determined I'd told all I had to tell.

And Roanna, what would they do with Roanna? Not kill her, surely. A horrible thought reared up in my mind — Roanna as part of the conspiracy, playing along as fellow victim, waiting to get me alone so I would tell her everything, not suspecting she belonged to the Aylmers first and to me not at all. Perhaps even now she was drinking hot coffee, laughing with Harry about how they'd all fooled me.

If I could just stay alive for ten, twelve hours. Then killing me would be quite unnecessary, would just add another charge to all the others. "Please," I said, "you think I'm someone else. You're wrong. I'm just *me*."

"Red Wolf," said Moreen. "That name meant nothing to" — she glared at her son — "to Jen, but it meant something to you."

I shook my head, as though bemused.

"And straight after you hear the name, you're desperate to find a phone, so desperate you ask Sebastian Bennett to find you a mobile when you find the others don't work."

Seb. I felt a wave of regret. I had thought him a friend. "I wanted to call my mum," I said. "That's all." Looking into Moreen Aylmer's eyes, I threw up my hands in a gesture of complete despair. "This is a nightmare," I said, sounding near to tears.

Behind me, Quint laughed softly. "You ain't seen nothing yet."

"Quint, be quiet." He subsided. "Now, Denise, be reasonable. Tell us everything you know, and that will be the end of it. I imagine you've concealed a message somewhere. We'll need that. And we need to know everyone you've spoken to, of course." She turned to her son. "Jen is no problem, I trust?"

"No problem," he said quickly.

"Sebastian can ask around, see if Denise has spread any wild tales. I'm concerned about the

157

bartender, Pete. Check him out closely. They seemed to have been on very good terms, and he spends time with Roanna."

"Roanna," said Quint with scorn. "She talks too much to too many people."

His mother gave him a icy look. "And *you* don't?" She swung back to me. "And you spoke with that private detective, Biddy Gallagher. What did you tell her?"

"Gallagher's a drunk," said Quint. "No one would listen to anything she said about anything."

"Maybe so, but she's been far too interested in Lainie Snead." To me she said accusingly, "You tried to strike up a conversation with Lainie, too, didn't you?"

I felt violated. They'd been watching me, listening to me. I'd suspected that I was under surveillance, but somehow it had never seemed quite real. I was sure it had begun when Roanna showed an interest in me. Controlling an almost overwhelming impulse to tell these two bastards what I thought of them, I said meekly, "Seeing Mr. Snead's widow was so upset, I just said something kind to her. I mean, it was awful what had happened to her husband."

"Lainie won't be talking to anyone," said Quint with confidence. "And I've persuaded her that any attempt to sue the resort would inevitably lead to serious accidents to her nearest and dearest." He laughed lightly. "I was very convincing. Lainie understood perfectly."

The door opened behind me. I tensed, ready to take advantage of any change in the situation, but Quint didn't look to see who it was. He kept the shotgun pointed at me.

"The wind's dropping," said George Aylmer.

As Denise Hunter would, I turned to him in entreaty. "Mr. Aylmer! Please. Can you help me? There's been some misunderstanding."

He ignored me, his attention wholly on his formidable wife. George Aylmer didn't look evil, or even severe. He was merely a middle-aged, slightly stooped man with the peevish attitude of one inconvenienced by the storm. "Moreen? What do you think about the chances of making the mainland in this weather? I'd like to be rid of our guest as soon as possible."

For a moment I thought that by *guest* he meant me, but of course he meant Red Wolf.

Moreen was incisive. "The catamaran can handle very heavy seas. Tell our guest that Quint will be along in five minutes to take him down to the dock." She consulted her watch, a small gold item worth, no doubt, a great deal of money. "There's still ample time for the project to be accomplished."

The project she referred to was almost certainly an attempt to assassinate the President. I had the comforting knowledge that the alert I'd sent about Red Wolf would mean that all presidential plans for sightseeing would be canceled and that Red Wolf's target was on his way back to the States. That is, if my e-mails had got through. If they hadn't . . .

At last George Aylmer appeared to notice I was in the room. "What'll we do with her?"

"Eddie took Ro along to have a little heart-to-heart with Harry," said Quint, "but I'm sure Eddie would jump at the chance of spending some time with Denise." He gave me a lighthearted grin. "He'll get you talking. You'll want to tell him everything."

I remained silent, the very picture, I hoped, of terror and confusion. There was no doubt in my mind that I was to be killed, otherwise nothing about Red Wolf or his plans would have been discussed in front of me. I was to be beaten, or worse, until I told everything useful, and then I'd be eliminated. And what cover story would they use? That I'd been swept out to sea? Battered on the coral until I was almost unrecognizable? Or perhaps my body would never be found.

Anger was giving me strength, revving me up until I knew that I would act at the first opportunity. I wasn't going to die. I'd have at least one chance, and I'd seize it. If it didn't work out, at least I'd be quickly dead. That way I'd escape slow torture, followed by the inevitable execution.

Moreen went to the desk and punched a key on the intercom. "Harry? Send Eddie here immediately. Quint is to escort our guest to the mainland. Keep Roanna with you. I'll speak with her myself, a little later." Her tone made it clear this conversation would not be a pleasant one.

George left the room without another glance at me. Quint, jogging from foot to foot, kept me under close scrutiny. "You sure the cat's safe?" he asked his mother. "It's bloody rough out there."

"The captain's expert. That's why I hired her."

Quint moved his shoulders, obviously uneasy about the crossing. "I suppose it's not that far."

"You're not landing at the usual place, Quint. That's poor security, and you should know that." She sounded disappointed in him, and he responded with a sulky expression. "The captain's been instructed to go down the coast quite a way, and drop off our passenger at an abandoned wharf, where he'll be met. That's where our responsibility ends."

I felt my shoulders slump. There wasn't time or people to cover every landing possibility on this section of the Queensland coast. It would be like every other time: Red Wolf would slip away, and his mythical image, that drew so many radicals to support him, would be enhanced.

Jeez, I thought. *Not me. I'm not hero material, so no one can expect me to do anything about it.* Anyway, what could I do? If I escaped my captors, I planned to hide until the authorities landed on the island and took over.

Identify the enemy, my trainer whispered in my ear. I almost nodded, listening to this advice. If I could see Red Wolf's face, even for a moment, and estimate his height, his build, even his ethnic background, then I could offer tangible information with which to hunt him down.

Eddie came in, the Smith & Wesson still clutched in his right hand.

"I'll say good-bye," said Quint. "We won't be meeting again."

CHAPTER FOURTEEN

Perhaps Quint had given some hostage-keeping
hints to Eddie Trebonus. Whatever the reason, he kept
his distance from me, and the wicked barrel of the
black automatic stayed trained on my stomach. He'd
shed his flapping dark raincoat, to reveal a garish
Hawaiian shirt and crumpled brown trousers.

"After you," he said to me, in a parody of good
manners.

I saw Moreen Aylmer frown at the dirt Eddie had
tracked in on his wet shoes. "Hurry up," she said,
obviously wanting him off her white carpet.

Out in the courtyard the rain had almost stopped, but the wind still keened. "Where's Roanna?" I asked.

"Shut up," he said without heat.

I shut up. I was going to get away from Eddie, or die trying, and I couldn't imagine dying. The blood sang in my veins, and I felt like an athlete about to run a race.

He indicated the way I was to go, out of the courtyard and toward a couple of squat, windowless buildings that were probably used for equipment storage.

Raising my voice above the storm, I asked over my shoulder, "Are you going to hurt me?"

"Sweetheart, I'm going to make you scream your lungs out," he said.

"I thought you liked me."

"Oh, I do. And I'm going to show you how much."

I stopped, turned to face him. There was a cocky tilt to his head, and his loose mouth was stretched in an anticipatory smile. With a jolt of disgust I noticed the bulge in his pants. Violence against a defenseless woman was obviously a turnon for Eddie.

He jiggled the gun in his hand. "Get a move on." When I looked around, a desperate animal at bay, he chuckled. "Don't bother," he crowed. "You aren't getting away from me."

I went on a few steps, then stumbled and fell hard, face down. "I've hurt my knee."

Eddie stood above me, just where I wanted him. "Get up," he said.

I rolled over, wincing, turned until I was supported on my left elbow, my right leg drawn up. "I don't think I can get up."

"Bitch," he said, bringing back one foot to kick me.

163

I went for his kneecap, the full force of my bent leg, released, hitting like a hammer. I heard the bone break. The wind snatched his scream as he went down, still clutching the gun.

I was up faster than thought, faster than I had ever been in training, totally focused on the gun. Eddie was in agony, but he'd transcended that. He wanted to kill me for doing this to him. In what seemed slow motion, the barrel began to swing my way.

My second kick, delivered with every bit of strength I had, was aimed at his face. I hit him cleanly above his upper lip, the follow-through smashing his nose. I felt the shock of the blow through my wet sneaker and up into by shin. I'd been shown the move many times, but never thought I'd ever use it, because, well-executed, the shards of bone were driven into the brain.

Eddie fell back, groaned, just once. His fingers relaxed, and the automatic slid slowly onto the wet ground.

Having no time for any better attempt at concealment, I dragged his body, with great effort, behind the nearest clump of bushes. Kneeling beside him, I felt for a pulse in his neck. I couldn't find one. I sat back on my heels, looking at his slack face. Water from the leaves was dripping into his half-open eyes, but of course he didn't blink. Eddie would never blink again.

I'd never killed anyone before, but I didn't feel anything at all. The one thought that tumbled through my mind was that Eddie Trebonus had ordered his last cocktail.

* * * * *

I was Alice in Wonderland's white rabbit, always in a hurry, always finding I had no time. I ran like that fictional rabbit for the dock where I hoped the catamaran still tugged at her moorings. I had Eddie's gun clamped in my hand, its lethal weight a reassurance.

Odd splatters were falling, but the rain had eased off, at least for the moment. The wind, however, screamed like banshees wailing for Eddie's soul. I shuddered. Maybe killing him was going to hit me hard, when I could sit and think about it.

Crouched by Eddie's body, I'd had a moment's debate about Oscar Fallon. If I had known where he was, I would have tried to release him, as two of us had a better chance than one. But looking for Fallon would have taken precious minutes, and increased the chance that I would be recaptured. Besides, I didn't know what condition he was in. Perhaps he was dead. It was better to leave the CIA man and go for the catamaran.

I ran past Roanna's little house, its lights still glowing a welcome. Inside it would be warm and dry, with the pan full of congealed egg still sitting on the stove. Bizarrely, I tried to remember if Roanna had started making the toast before Eddie came bursting through the door.

Then I was through the security gate and pounding along the private path where Roanna and I had strolled in the sunlight. It seemed weeks, months ago, but it had only been two days before. I slowed when I came to the shore, stopping in the shelter of the little dive shop to get my breath. The waves were ferocious, pounding the sand with heavy blows, and hissing right up and into the greenery edging the beach.

With relief I saw that the catamaran was still there, tethered with double moorings fore and aft, and bucking violently in the high seas. She'd been reversed in, so that she pointed her bows directly into the lines of angry waves. On the dock a single light atop a metal pole trembled with the shock of the heaving water and the power of the wind.

There was no one to see me. I could see the lights of the hotel winking through the thrashing trees. Guests would be snug in their rooms, perhaps sharing with people who had to abandon the little cabanas that now had salt water swirling around them. I had a sudden vision of my bland little beige room with its generic furniture, and wished with all my heart that I was safe there, with nothing to worry about except my next shift at the Tropical Heat.

I'd moved to the beginning of the dock when someone got off the vessel. It was the captain, her slicker whipping around her. Quint Aylmer followed her, gesturing emphatically. She swung around, pointing first at the sea, and then at the sky. The waves were huge, rolling in to pitch the cat violently. I could see why the captain didn't want to risk it. I had the craven hope that she would, and perhaps fate would take a hand. The catamaran would sink, and Red Wolf would choke his life out in a shallow tropical sea, so there'd be no need for me to worry that I'd done nothing to stop him leaving the island.

I ducked under the dock's wooden supports for cover. Under the walkway the wild water surged, alternately sucking and battering the sand, which seemed to dissolve under me so I had trouble keeping my footing. On the opposite side to the catamaran a lower platform had been built to accommodate small launches. If I could crouch on the steps leading up to the main walkway, I'd be close to the cat and might be able to see something. I rammed the gun tightly in the waistband of the jeans I wore — Roanna's jeans. I'd checked the magazine: eight rounds and one in the firing chamber. Nine shots in all. I wasn't going to start an effective war with armament like this.

Earlier I'd been soaked to the skin by rain, and now it was salty ocean. I waded, waist high, the force of the swirling water terrifying in its intensity. I was slammed against a pylon, nearly pulled under, but I struggled, one ponderous step at a time, clutching at every handhold I could find, until I could grab the slippery bottom step of the platform. I crawled up on hands and knees, pathetically grateful to be out of the ravening sea, my eyes screwed up against the stinging spray.

As I came to the top of the steps I folded myself into the smallest package possible, raising my head just high enough to look over the edge. Close by me the captain and Quint were still arguing. I caught a few of her words not snatched by the storm. "...the seas too high. Suicide to ..."

Quint, mercifully without shotgun, yelled back at her. "We're going! You haven't any choice!"

Then a man, small, insignificant, leapt from the cat and strode toward the two of them. He wore a baseball cap and dark clothes. The captain shrank back, as though he were of figure of menace.

And of course he was. Red Wolf.

I strained to see his face, but the bobbing light

above was ineffectual, and the brim of his cap threw a dark shadow across his features. The gun hung heavy at my waist. I was close enough for a clear shot. I began to shake, my teeth chattering. I'd already killed one person tonight. This wasn't like the movies, where heroes dispatched villains with aplomb. Right now I couldn't even be sure I could pull the trigger, let alone aim the gun.

The argument was over; the captain jumped back onto the heaving vessel, followed by the two men. A few moments later Quint and a crewman appeared, each with a machete. Above the thunder of the surf I heard the cat's engines roar, and saw a plume of steam from the exhaust. Quint went to the bow, the other man to the stern. The crewman signaled, and simultaneously they slashed the mooring lines. Released, the cat barely held her own, poised with engines straining against the might of the running sea. White water broke over the vessel, foaming along the decks. I saw Quint and the crewman clinging to the railings as they struggled inside.

I'd missed the opportunity that every national security force in the West would have wanted me to take. In those few seconds, I could have executed a mass murderer, a man who had sown terror throughout the world. A rush of shame filled me.

I hardly realized what I was doing, or why, but as the catamaran began at last to move away from the dock, I found myself straightening, bursting from my hiding place. The black water yawned beneath, and then I was leaping the widening gap, slipping, falling, onto the narrow side deck of the cat, my elbow fired with pain where I hit it on the railing.

It seemed impossible that I hadn't been seen, but no one appeared to challenge me. On my knees, water surging around me, I wrenched the gun from my waistband. The thought skated through my mind that it was standard practice to hold this weapon with both hands, but with the slippery surface pitching beneath me, I needed at least one hand free to stop myself from being swept over the side into the hungry ocean.

I looked back. The light on the dock was receding into darkness as the cat picked up speed. Ahead, steps, dimly illuminated, led up to the bridge. Red Wolf would be there with the others, all of them willing the laboring vessel to keep her bows pointed square into the swell. It would be fatal if she wallowed, so that the waves could hit her broadside and break her back.

I made it to the steel steps, slammed my knee against the first one when the cat made a sickening downward plunge, then crawled up the others, clinging with my left hand, the automatic clenched tightly in my right. For visibility, the bridge was surrounded by windows, but now spray streamed across the glass in torrents. Like an orphan in a storm, I peered into the lighted area, and saw his face clearly for the first time.

He was standing beside the captain, feet spread, keeping his balance on the pitching floor with apparent ease. He'd taken off his cap, and through the distortion of the wet glass he looked ordinary, normal. A face you'd see in a thousand rooms, a thousand streets. Just a man, clean-shaven, of no particular nationality or definite age. Everyman, set to destroy the fabric of the political world.

I stared at Red Wolf, memorizing him as though he

were an observation test. Quint stood next to him, and I used that to estimate his height. Shorter than me, lightly built, with hands large for his slight frame.

Suddenly aware of the automatic clenched in my hand, I measured my chance of getting a good shot at him. It was possible, but it was likely to be a suicide mission. Besides Red Wolf, I would have to take down three — Quint, a crewman and the captain. And with no one at the helm, the cat would be at the mercy of the sea.

I squeezed my eyes shut, seeing sunlight and the faces of people I loved. I opened my eyes, cool, determined. I'd do it.

The decision was taken from me. Quint turned his head and looked in my direction. I saw his mouth drop open, then he was pointing, shouting. The captain swung her head around, startled. I jumped away from the window as the catamaran smacked into a huge wave. She shuddered, staggered, bows down, then rose up, up, until I skidded backward down the metal steps.

My head hit the deck. I had a blurred impression of someone vaulting down from the bridge, then Quint was on me. I'd lost the gun. His weight on my chest, I turned my head, frantic to find it. Its compact black shape slid out of reach, then dropped over into the sea.

Quint had me by the throat. His face contorted, he slammed my head on the deck. He was screaming "Cunt!" over and over again. I went for his eyes, and he jerked his head back.

Over his shoulder I saw the dark shape of a monstrous wave looming, curling with open mouth to devour us all. Locked together in an obscene embrace,

Quint and I were buried in an avalanche of water, then as the cat yawed, we were swept helplessly into the boiling sea.

I surfaced, gasping for air. I had a confused impression that Quint had clutched at me as we had been pulled down, but the current had torn me away from him. I looked around, frantic to find the catamaran. I caught a glimpse of her lights, as, mortally wounded, she slid sideways down the side of a breaking wave. Then everything was dark and I was alone in black sea, fighting for every breath, tossed like a tiny cork on an infinite ocean.

Swimming was not an option; just keeping my head above the surface took every bit of energy I had. If the cat had cleared the island, then I was lost, there was no way I would survive long enough to be washed onto the mainland shore. I kicked off my shoes and jeans before their weight could drag me down, then concentrated on staying afloat.

All sense of time had left me. I was still wearing my watch, and ridiculously I squinted at it in the darkness. Would it be light soon? If I could see land, then I would have at least the hope that I might survive. It seemed to me that the sky was growing lighter, that the sea was becoming defined, its face more terrifying as I began to make out its ever-changing features.

Over the shriek of the wind I became conscious of a deep pounding. Surf, smashing against something substantial — rocks, or reefs, or sand. My frail body cringed. At least in the heaving water I was cushioned, tossed in a rough salt embrace, but the frenzied waves could pulp me against a hard surface.

A dark gray dawn was breaking over a fierce gray

ocean. Lifted high by a surge of water, I saw the line of breakers, and with a shock of joy realized that it was Aylmer Island, and that I was being swept toward the mangroves at the end of the beach. A surge of energy I didn't know I had got me swimming, my efforts laughable against the swell, but slowly I began to make headway.

Months, years later, it seemed, I was grabbing at mangrove trunks, uncaring as I was rammed against them, my skin abraded by rough surfaces. I crawled on hands and knees out of the water, out of the mangroves, and sank, panting, onto a tangled mess of vegetation left by the storm at the margin of the beach. No opulent couch could feel more luxurious.

I tried to sit up. There was something farther along in the mangrove trees, something driven by the sea deep into their embrace. I couldn't imagine why I hadn't seen it before. Like a broken toy, the catamaran lay on her side, one pontoon split and gaping.

I tried to get up. Someone had to look for Red Wolf. I was conscious someone had come up behind me. I looked vainly for a weapon, then turned to face the threat.

"Jesus, Denise," said Pete. "I reckon you're to blame for the fact the island's now a military camp."

CHAPTER FIFTEEN

I was on leave, sitting in a four-wheel drive over-looking the wonderful scenery of Tasmania's most famous national park. The peak of Cradle Mountain rose above us, birds called to each other, wildflowers bloomed. The two other tourists who shared the vehicle with me were chatting to the driver, exclaiming over the beauties outside. One, a cheerful American with one of those Southern accents that sound put on but aren't, clicked away with his elaborate camera as he talked.

I wanted silence, so I climbed out of the vehicle

and wandered away to lean against the massive trunk of a eucalyptus that soared high into the cloudless sky. It had seemed a good idea to get away, after the pressure of the past months, so I had found a small guided tour and had booked myself on it. The fact that Tasmania was an island state was somewhat ironic, as I wished I were on another island altogether. A much smaller one, and more than two thousand kilometers to the north. I could shut my eyes and see the curve of the beach, the coconut palms swaying, the line of Roanna's jaw . . .

Let it go, Denise.

The arrests were accomplished, the furor in the media abating as other sensational stories took center stage. There'd be another huge boost to the story when the trials began, but that was a long time off, as the evidence was scattered in a dozen countries.

I'd been debriefed so often I was tired of telling my story. The one amusing point was when I met Oscar Fallon, not, of course, his real name. He'd been furious that he hadn't been informed that an ASIO plant was on the island, and didn't even relax his grim expression when I pointed out with a sunny smile that it was only fair, since the Central Intelligence Bureau had neglected to tell ASIO that *he* was there. Fallon had been undercover as part of a CIA investigation of Lloyd Snead's activities, and had had the embarrassment of having the target of his assignment murdered under his very nose. But I suspected that the real reason Oscar was miffed had to do with the fact that I had gained the lion's share of the attention, because I was the only agent who had seen Red Wolf up close and could identify him.

Red Wolf. His body hadn't been found, and it was

assumed that he had remained aboard the crippled catamaran, along with the captain. The crewman had drowned — his body had been found — and the captain claimed that her passenger had been washed overboard too, but the general belief was that the terrorist had survived, both he and the captain staying with the craft as it was battered by the storm and then beached on the shore. Under arrest, she'd steadfastly refused to discuss the matter, claiming complete ignorance of his true identity. It seemed impossible that the man had yet again evaded capture, as within a few hours the island had been under military control, but by then Red Wolf had melted away, as though he had never been there at all.

Moreen, George and Harry Aylmer were being held without bail, the list of charges long: treason, murder, attempted murder, kidnaping, extortion, fraud, and, in a nice final touch, tax evasion.

Quint Aylmer had escaped justice: His body had been washed ashore on a mainland beach two days after the storm had blown itself out.

Cynthia Urquhart had been indicted for Snead's murder after Tony, the Aylmer sons' unpleasant friend, had rolled over for a lighter charge, freely giving evidence that he had tampered with Snead's scuba tanks at her request. She was also under investigation for other suspicious deaths in America and Canada. Seb, Bruce, and lesser players had all been charged with various offenses.

In future court appearances, I would be a witness for the prosecution against many of them. It was a daunting prospect, with trials stretching years into the future.

And Roanna? She remained free, as there was insufficient evidence to charge her. Dark comments from my superiors indicated the consensus was that she knew exactly what was going on but hadn't actively participated. I wasn't so sure, or perhaps I didn't want to believe that of her.

I'd seen Roanna that morning on the island when, so exhausted that I could hardly speak, I'd been interrogated by the military commander who had landed by helicopter with his commando force to secure the resort. I'd asked to meet with Roanna, and I'd been taken to the room where she was under guard. White-faced and drawn, she'd still smiled when she saw me. We hadn't been left alone, and we'd only spoken for a few minutes before I was whisked away to the mainland where agents were waiting to extract every particle of information I could give on Red Wolf.

I'd seen her twice more after that, both at committal hearings for her parents and brother Harry. We'd only exchanged a few words, but at the last one, just a few weeks ago, Roanna had impulsively put her hand on my arm and said, "I'm going back to the island to run the resort. Will you visit me sometime?"

Before I could reply, she'd shaken her head ruefully. "I'm sorry, that was stupid of me. I was just part of your job."

I had looked after her as she'd walked away, thinking how she had only known me as Denise Hunter, the not-so-expert bartender.

The tour guide broke into my thoughts. "Ready to move on, Den?" he said. "We've Twisted Lake to see before the sun goes down."

"I'll be a moment."

I turned my back on them and took out the little

cellular phone that had been my present to myself for my birthday. I didn't need to look up the number: I'd gone to punch it in a dozen times before and had stopped.

"Roanna?" I said. "It's Denise. Denise *Cleever*."

LOOKING FOR NAIAD?

Buy our books at
www.naiadpress.com

or call our toll-free number
1-800-533-1973

or by fax (24 hours a day)
1-850-539-9731

A few of the publications of
THE NAIAD PRESS, INC.
P.O. Box 10543   Tallahassee, Florida 32302
Phone (850) 539-5965
Toll-Free Order Number: 1-800-533-1973
Web Site: WWW.NAIADPRESS.COM
Mail orders welcome. Please include 15% postage.
Write or call for our free catalog which also features an
incredible selection of lesbian videos.

MURDER UNDERCOVER by Claire McNab. 192 pp. 1st Denise
Cleever thriller.   ISBN 1-56280-259-3 $11.95

EVERY TIME WE SAY GOODBYE by Jaye Maiman. 272 pp.
6th Robin Miller mystery.   ISBN 1-56280-248-8   11.95

SEVENTH HEAVEN by Kate Calloway. 224 pp. 7th Cassidy
James mystery.   ISBN 1-56280-262-3   11.95

STRANGERS IN THE NIGHT by Barbara Johnson. 208 pp. Her
body and soul react to a stranger's touch.   ISBN 1-56280-256-9   11.95

THE VERY THOUGHT OF YOU edited by Barbara Grier and
Christine Cassidy. 288 pp. Erotic love stories by Naiad Press
authors.   ISBN 1-56280-250-X   14.95

TO HAVE AND TO HOLD by Petty J. Herring. 192 pp. Their
friendship grows to intense passion . . .   ISBN 1-56280-251-8   11.95

INTIMATE STRANGER by Laura DeHart Young. 192 pp.
Ignoring Tray's myserious past, could Cole be playing with fire?
                                               ISBN 1-56280-249-6   11.95

SHATTERED ILLUSIONS by Kaye Davis. 256 pp. 4th
Maris Middleton mystery.   ISBN 1-56280-252-6   11.95

SETUP by Claire McNab. 224 pp. 11th Detective Inspector Carol
Ashton mystery.   ISBN 1-56280-255-0   11.95

THE DAWNING by Laura Adams. 224 pp. What if you had the
power to change the past?   ISBN 1-56280-246-1   11.95

NEVER ENDING by Marianne Martin. 224 pp. Temptation
appears in the form of an old friend and lover. ISBN 1-56280-247-X   11.95

ONE OF OUR OWN by Diane Salvatore. 240 pp. Carly Matson
has a secret. So does Lela Johns.   ISBN 1-56280-243-7   11.95

DOUBLE TAKEOUT by Tracey Richardson. 176 pp. 3rd Stevie
Houston mystery.   ISBN 1-56280-244-5   11.95

CAPTIVE HEART by Frankie J. Jones. 176 pp. Love in the
fast lane or heartside romance? ISBN 1-56280-258-5   11.95

WICKED GOOD TIME by Diana Tremain Braund. 224 pp. In
charge at work, out of control in her heart. ISBN 1-56280-241-0   11.95

SNAKE EYES by Pat Welch. 256 pp. 7th Helen Black mystery.
ISBN 1-56280-242-9   11.95

CHANGE OF HEART by Linda Hill. 176 pp. High fashion and
love in a glamorous world. ISBN 1-56280-238-0   11.95

UNSTRUNG HEART by Robbi Sommers. 176 pp. Putting life
in order again. ISBN 1-56280-239-9   11.95

BIRDS OF A FEATHER by Jackie Calhoun. 240 pp. Life begins
with love. ISBN 1-56280-240-2   11.95

THE DRIVE by Trisha Todd. 176 pp. The star of *Claire of the
Moon* tells all! ISBN 1-56280-237-2   11.95

BOTH SIDES by Saxon Bennett. 240 pp. A community of
women falling in and out of love. ISBN 1-56280-236-4   11.95

WATERMARK by Karin Kallmaker. 256 pp. One burning
question . . . how to lead her back to love? ISBN 1-56280-235-6   11.95

THE OTHER WOMAN by Ann O'Leary. 240 pp. Her roguish
way draws women like a magnet. ISBN 1-56280-234-8   11.95

SILVER THREADS by Lyn Denison.208 pp. Finding her way
back to love . . . ISBN 1-56280-231-3   11.95

CHIMNEY ROCK BLUES by Janet McClellan. 224 pp. 4th Tru
North mystery. ISBN 1-56280-233-X   11.95

OMAHA'S BELL by Penny Hayes. 208 pp. Orphaned Keeley
Delaney woos the lovely Prudence Morris. ISBN 1-56280-232-1   11.95

SIXTH SENSE by Kate Calloway. 224 pp. 6th Cassidy James
mystery. ISBN 1-56280-228-3   11.95

DAWN OF THE DANCE by Marianne K. Martin. 224 pp. A dance
with an old friend, nothing more . . . yeah! ISBN 1-56280-229-1   11.95

WEDDING BELL BLUES by Julia Watts. 240 pp. Love, family,
and a recipe for success. ISBN 1-56280-230-5   11.95

THOSE WHO WAIT by Peggy J. Herring. 160 pp. Two
sisters . . . in love with the same woman. ISBN 1-56280-223-2   11.95

WHISPERS IN THE WIND by Frankie J. Jones. 192 pp. "If you
don't want this," she whispered, "all you have to say is 'stop.' "
ISBN 1-56280-226-7   11.95

WHEN SOME BODY DISAPPEARS by Therese Szymanski.
192 pp. 3rd Brett Higgins mystery. ISBN 1-56280-227-5   11.95

THE WAY LIFE SHOULD BE by Diana Braund. 240 pp. Which
one will teach her the true meaning of love? ISBN 1-56280-221-6   11.95

UNTIL THE END by Kaye Davis. 256pp. 3rd Maris Middleton
mystery.   ISBN 1-56280-222-4   11.95

FIFTH WHEEL by Kate Calloway. 224 pp. 5th Cassidy James
mystery.   ISBN 1-56280-218-6   11.95

JUST YESTERDAY by Linda Hill. 176 pp. Reliving all the
passion of yesterday.   ISBN 1-56280-219-4   11.95

THE TOUCH OF YOUR HAND edited by Barbara Grier and
Christine Cassidy. 304 pp. Erotic love stories by Naiad Press
authors.   ISBN 1-56280-220-8   14.95

WINDROW GARDEN by Janet McClellan. 192 pp. They discover
a passion they never dreamed possible.   ISBN 1-56280-216-X   11.95

PAST DUE by Claire McNab. 224 pp. 10th Carol Ashton
mystery.   ISBN 1-56280-217-8   11.95

CHRISTABEL by Laura Adams. 224 pp. Two captive hearts and
the passion that will set them free.   ISBN 1-56280-214-3   11.95

PRIVATE PASSIONS by Laura DeHart Young. 192 pp. An
unforgettable new portrait of lesbian love . . .   ISBN 1-56280-215-1   11.95

BAD MOON RISING by Barbara Johnson. 208 pp. 2nd Colleen
Fitzgerald mystery.   ISBN 1-56280-211-9   11.95

RIVER QUAY by Janet McClellan. 208 pp. 3rd Tru North
mystery.   ISBN 1-56280-212-7   11.95

ENDLESS LOVE by Lisa Shapiro. 272 pp. To believe, once
again, that love can be forever.   ISBN 1-56280-213-5   11.95

FALLEN FROM GRACE by Pat Welch. 256 pp. 6th Helen Black
mystery.   ISBN 1-56280-209-7   11.95

THE NAKED EYE by Catherine Ennis. 208 pp. Her lover in the
camera's eye . . .   ISBN 1-56280-210-0   11.95

OVER THE LINE by Tracey Richardson. 176 pp. 2nd Stevie
Houston mystery.   ISBN 1-56280-202-X   11.95

JULIA'S SONG by Ann O'Leary. 208 pp. Strangely
disturbing . . . strangely exciting.   ISBN 1-56280-197-X   11.95

LOVE IN THE BALANCE by Marianne K. Martin. 256 pp.
Weighing the costs of love . . .   ISBN 1-56280-199-6   11.95

PIECE OF MY HEART by Julia Watts. 208 pp. All the
stuff that dreams are made of —   ISBN 1-56280-206-2   11.95

MAKING UP FOR LOST TIME by Karin Kallmaker. 240 pp.
Nobody does it better . . .   ISBN 1-56280-196-1   11.95

GOLD FEVER by Lyn Denison. 224 pp. By author of *Dream
Lover*.   ISBN 1-56280-201-1   11.95

WHEN THE DEAD SPEAK by Therese Szymanski. 224 pp. 2nd
Brett Higgins mystery.   ISBN 1-56280-198-8   11.95

FOURTH DOWN by Kate Calloway. 240 pp. 4th Cassidy James
mystery.   ISBN 1-56280-205-4   11.95

A MOMENT'S INDISCRETION by Peggy J. Herring. 176 pp.
There's a fine line between love and lust . . .   ISBN 1-56280-194-5   11.95

CITY LIGHTS/COUNTRY CANDLES by Penny Hayes. 208 pp.
About the women she has known . . .   ISBN 1-56280-195-3   11.95

POSSESSIONS by Kaye Davis. 240 pp. 2nd Maris Middleton
mystery.   ISBN 1-56280-192-9   11.95

A QUESTION OF LOVE by Saxon Bennett. 208 pp. Every
woman is granted one great love.   ISBN 1-56280-205-4   11.95

RHYTHM TIDE by Frankie J. Jones. 160 pp.   . . . to desire
passionately and be passionately desired.   ISBN 1-56280-189-9   11.95

PENN VALLEY PHOENIX by Janet McClellan. 208 pp. 2nd
Tru North Mystery.   ISBN 1-56280-200-3   11.95

BY RESERVATION ONLY by Jackie Calhoun. 240 pp. A
chance for true happiness.   ISBN 1-56280-191-0   11.95

OLD BLACK MAGIC by Jaye Maiman. 272 pp. 9th Robin
Miller mystery.   ISBN 1-56280-175-9   11.95

LEGACY OF LOVE by Marianne K. Martin. 240 pp. Women
will do anything for her . . .   ISBN 1-56280-184-8   11.95

LETTING GO by Ann O'Leary. 160 pp. Laura, at 39, in love
with 23-year-old Kate.   ISBN 1-56280-183-X   11.95

LADY BE GOOD edited by Barbara Grier and Christine Cassidy.
288 pp. Erotic stories by Naiad Press authors.   ISBN 1-56280-180-5   14.95

CHAIN LETTER by Claire McNab. 288 pp. 9th Carol Ashton
mystery.   ISBN 1-56280-181-3   11.95

NIGHT VISION by Laura Adams. 256 pp. Erotic fantasy romance
by "famous" author.   ISBN 1-56280-182-1   11.95

SEA TO SHINING SEA by Lisa Shapiro. 256 pp. Unable to resist
the raging passion . . .   ISBN 1-56280-177-5   11.95

THIRD DEGREE by Kate Calloway. 224 pp. 3rd Cassidy James
mystery.   ISBN 1-56280-185-6   11.95

WHEN THE DANCING STOPS by Therese Szymanski. 272 pp.
1st Brett Higgins mystery.   ISBN 1-56280-186-4   11.95

PHASES OF THE MOON by Julia Watts. 192 pp. . . . . hungry
for everything life has to offer.   ISBN 1-56280-176-7   11.95

BABY IT'S COLD by Jaye Maiman. 256 pp. 5th Robin Miller
mystery.   ISBN 1-56280-156-2   10.95

CLASS REUNION by Linda Hill. 176 pp. The girl from her
past . . . .   ISBN 1-56280-178-3   11.95

DREAM LOVER by Lyn Denison. 224 pp. A soft, sensuous,
romantic fantasy.   ISBN 1-56280-173-1   11.95

FORTY LOVE by Diana Simmonds. 288 pp. Joyous, heart-warming romance.   ISBN 1-56280-171-6   11.95

IN THE MOOD by Robbi Sommers. 160 pp. The queen of erotic tension!   ISBN 1-56280-172-4   11.95

SWIMMING CAT COVE by Lauren Douglas. 192 pp. 2nd Allison O'Neil Mystery.   ISBN 1-56280-168-6   11.95

THE LOVING LESBIAN by Claire McNab and Sharon Gedan. 240 pp. Explore the experiences that make lesbian love unique.
                                                         ISBN 1-56280-169-4   14.95

COURTED by Celia Cohen. 160 pp. Sparkling romantic encounter.   ISBN 1-56280-166-X   11.95

SEASONS OF THE HEART by Jackie Calhoun. 240 pp. Romance through the years.   ISBN 1-56280-167-8   11.95

K. C. BOMBER by Janet McClellan. 208 pp. 1st Tru North mystery.   ISBN 1-56280-157-0   11.95

LAST RITES by Tracey Richardson. 192 pp. 1st Stevie Houston mystery.   ISBN 1-56280-164-3   11.95

EMBRACE IN MOTION by Karin Kallmaker. 256 pp. A whirlwind love affair.   ISBN 1-56280-165-1   11.95

HOT CHECK by Peggy J. Herring. 192 pp. Will workaholic Alice fall for guitarist Ricky?   ISBN 1-56280-163-5   11.95

OLD TIES by Saxon Bennett. 176 pp. Can Cleo surrender to a passionate new love?   ISBN 1-56280-159-7   11.95

LOVE ON THE LINE by Laura DeHart Young. 176 pp. Will Stef win Kay's heart?   ISBN 1-56280-162-7   11.95

DEVIL'S LEG CROSSING by Kaye Davis. 192 pp. 1st Maris Middleton mystery.   ISBN 1-56280-158-9   11.95

COSTA BRAVA by Marta Balletbo Coll. 144 pp. Read the book, see the movie!   ISBN 1-56280-153-8   11.95

MEETING MAGDALENE & OTHER STORIES by Marilyn Freeman. 144 pp. Read the book, see the movie!
                                                         ISBN 1-56280-170-8   11.95

SECOND FIDDLE by Kate 208 pp. 2nd P.I. Cassidy James mystery.   ISBN 1-56280-169-6   11.95

LAUREL by Isabel Miller. 128 pp. By the author of the beloved *Patience and Sarah*.   ISBN 1-56280-146-5   10.95

LOVE OR MONEY by Jackie Calhoun. 240 pp. The romance of real life.   ISBN 1-56280-147-3   10.95

SMOKE AND MIRRORS by Pat Welch. 224 pp. 5th Helen Black Mystery.   ISBN 1-56280-143-0   10.95

DANCING IN THE DARK edited by Barbara Grier & Christine
Cassidy. 272 pp. Erotic love stories by Naiad Press authors.
ISBN 1-56280-144-9   14.95

TIME AND TIME AGAIN by Catherine Ennis. 176 pp. Passionate
love affair.   ISBN 1-56280-145-7   10.95

PAXTON COURT by Diane Salvatore. 256 pp. Erotic and wickedly
funny contemporary tale about the business of learning to live
together.   ISBN 1-56280-114-7   10.95

INNER CIRCLE by Claire McNab. 208 pp. 8th Carol Ashton
Mystery.   ISBN 1-56280-135-X   11.95

LESBIAN SEX: AN ORAL HISTORY by Susan Johnson.
240 pp. Need we say more?   ISBN 1-56280-142-2   14.95

WILD THINGS by Karin Kallmaker. 240 pp. By the undisputed
mistress of lesbian romance.   ISBN 1-56280-139-2   11.95

THE GIRL NEXT DOOR by Mindy Kaplan. 208 pp. Just what
you d expect.   ISBN 1-56280-140-6   11.95

NOW AND THEN by Penny Hayes. 240 pp. Romance on the
westward journey.   ISBN 1-56280-121-X   11.95

HEART ON FIRE by Diana Simmonds. 176 pp. The romantic and
erotic rival of *Curious Wine*.   ISBN 1-56280-152-X   11.95

DEATH AT LAVENDER BAY by Lauren Wright Douglas. 208 pp.
1st Allison O'Neil Mystery.   ISBN 1-56280-085-X   11.95

YES I SAID YES I WILL by Judith McDaniel. 272 pp. Hot
romance by famous author.   ISBN 1-56280-138-4   11.95

FORBIDDEN FIRES by Margaret C. Anderson. Edited by Mathilda
Hills. 176 pp. Famous author's "unpublished" Lesbian romance.
ISBN 1-56280-123-6   21.95

SIDE TRACKS by Teresa Stores. 160 pp. Gender-bending
Lesbians on the road.   ISBN 1-56280-122-8   10.95

WILDWOOD FLOWERS by Julia Watts. 208 pp. Hilarious and
heart-warming tale of true love.   ISBN 1-56280-127-9   10.95

NEVER SAY NEVER by Linda Hill. 224 pp. Rule #1: Never get
involved with . . .   ISBN 1-56280-126-0   11.95

THE WISH LIST by Saxon Bennett. 192 pp. Romance through
the years.   ISBN 1-56280-125-2   10.95

These are just a few of the many Naiad Press titles — we are the oldest and
largest lesbian/feminist publishing company in the world. We also offer an
enormous selection of lesbian video products. Please request a complete
catalog. We offer personal service; we encourage and welcome direct mail
orders from individuals who have limited access to bookstores carrying our
publications.